Vicky Grut

Live Show, Drink Included

Collected Stories

Holland Park Press London

Published by Holland Park Press 2018

Copyright © Vicky Grut 2018

First Edition

A CIP catalogue record for this book is
available from The British Library.

ISBN 978-1-907320-79-8

Cover designed by Reactive Graphics

Printed and bound by
CPI Group (UK) Ltd, Croydon CR0 4YY

www.hollandparkpress.co.uk

To Bill

For the stories in this collection Vicky Grut takes inspiration from a range of often ordinary situations and explores how easily things can go awry or take an unexpected turn. The stories veer from the realistic to the surreal, and nothing is quite what it seems.

For example, an office worker is ordered to step away from her office desk by slightly sinister inspectors. An academic's impulsive reaction to being mistaken for a shop assistant lands her in big trouble. A young couple are in for a bit of a surprise when they decide on the spur of the moment to visit a Soho sex-show.

Be prepared to be not only entertained but also taken by surprise when reading the fourteen mini-novels in this collection.

CONTENTS

A few minutes before I was due to take my midmorning break, four strangers walked into the office. One of the men stayed at the door while the others went over to Sondra, our office manager. I watched them out of the corner of my eye. They all wore white shirts and navy blue suits; the woman was in a skirt. From head office, I thought. There was an undercurrent of controlled purpose to their movements that I didn't like. They spoke in low voices.

Sondra stood up. At first she appeared to be challenging them. 'Who authorized this?' I heard her say.

I began to work my feet back into my shoes under the desk while keeping my gaze fixed on Sondra. I reached for my bag, slipped the strap over my shoulder. I could see the lobby from where I sat. I could be away in less than a minute.

Just then, Elaine came scuttling down from Accounts with a sheaf of papers in one hand. She brushed past the man at the door without even noticing him and headed for Phil, who orders our stationery. She waved the document, tapping at something with her pencil. 'What's this, Phil? What's this?!'

Sondra stepped out into the centre of the room. 'OK team!' She looked around at all twenty of us sitting at our desks. 'I want you to finish what you're doing right now – end your call, save your data, whatever it might be – and then I'd like you to go either to the left or to the right and stand along the wall. Take nothing with you. Your handbags, mobiles, iPads must be left out on the desks in plain view.'

A murmur of confusion rippled through the room.

'Why?' somebody asked.

'Please comply with your supervisor's instructions,' said one of the be-suited men. 'We'll do our best to get through this as quickly and smoothly as possible.'

'Get through what?'

I'd heard enough. Gripping the strap of my bag with one hand I rose smoothly and headed out towards the lifts.

The man at the door stepped out to bar my way. 'If you wouldn't mind waiting a bit, please, Miss.' He waved me back.

'It's my break now,' I said. 'I need to go to the toilet.' As I spoke, I did indeed feel an urgent need to pee. Nerves, I thought, though of course I had nothing to be nervous about.

The man shook his head. 'No one is authorized to leave this room at the moment. We'll get through this as quickly as we can.' He didn't meet my eye. His words were directed at a spot somewhere above my head, as if he couldn't spare the time to look at me directly, as if he had more important things to see.

The blue-skirted woman came over and marched me to the left-hand side of the room, adding me to a cluster that was beginning to form around the drinking fountain.

'That bag needs to be on your desk,' she said. 'I'll pop it back for you, shall I?' The words were pleasant enough but the tone was chilly.

'I'll do it,' I said.

'No. I want you to stay right there. Just tell me which desk is yours.'

Reluctantly I surrendered my handbag and pointed out my desk.

'We appreciate your cooperation,' one of the men said in a robotic tone.

Blue-Skirt deposited my bag and rejoined her colleagues who were working their way down the lines of desks, accompanied by a worried-looking Sondra.

From the opposite side of the room came a flurry of noise and movement. Elaine from Accounts was attempting to break out.

'How many times do I have to explain, I *must* get back upstairs?! We have heaps to do. The auditor wants our figures by 4 p.m.!'

The suits pushed her back but Elaine wouldn't give up. 'We're busy beyond belief today!' she kept repeating. 'Beyond belief!'

Blue-Skirt said something to Sondra, who unlocked one of the meeting rooms at the back of the office and Elaine was ushered away, out of sight. The rest of us watched this scene in uneasy silence.

Roxanna, who deals with website queries, murmured, 'What do you think they're looking for?'

'Who cares!' cried Liz, my nearest desk neighbour. 'If they want to pay me to stand around doing nothing I'm not going to complain.'

Some people laughed, including me. Liz comes closest to being what I'd call a friend. She showed me round when I joined the company, filled me in on all the unwritten rules, explained what was tolerated and what was not. If I get stuck she's always helpful as long as she's not under too much pressure.

'All I need now to improve my mood is a piña colada,' said Bob – still scorched and lazy from a week in Tenerife.

But others were looking anxious. There must have been a leak, someone said, or an error. Something had probably been done or not done, and the team had been sent down from head office to find the leak or the error, or the thing done or not – perhaps all of these.

'We don't know what they know,' said Andrea, a milk-pale woman newly appointed to the sales team. 'They're probably not allowed to tell us why they're doing this.' I'd heard a rumour that she'd been unemployed for more than a year and had applied for three hundred and fifty jobs before getting this one. Three hundred and fifty rejections: it didn't bear thinking about.

People began to mutter about Elaine. Why did she have to make a fuss and soak up the time of not just one but *two* of the suits, who would otherwise have been continuing their search of the desks. 'They might even have finished

13

by now,' someone muttered, 'if it wasn't for *her*.'

Bob mentioned that he'd always found Elaine a bit demanding. Sometimes he felt she enjoyed pulling rank – always talking about the auditor this, the auditor that. 'Who's even *seen* this so-called auditor?' Bob scratched at his sunburn.

Derek, who'd been in the customer service team for years, leapt to Elaine's defence. It was shameful the way these strangers were treating her. 'She's probably worked here longer than all of us lot put together.' He said he thought it was a symptom of the way things had changed since the takeover.

'Yeah,' said Liz, 'bloody French.'

No, no, the French company lost the bid, said Derek, we'd been bought by a German firm. Indeed not, said someone else, the money behind the takeover was from China. 'I heard it was Americans,' said Roxanna.

'Well, whoever they are, I think it's wrong,' said Derek.

'Tell you what, though,' said Liz, 'we're lucky to have kept our jobs – in the current climate.' Her words rippled through the group like a Siberian breeze. We all fell silent. Some glanced over at Andrea, who was staring at the carpet. Three hundred and fifty rejections; you didn't need to experience that to fear it.

At last the meeting-room door opened and the blue-suited man and the woman appeared with Elaine between them. She seemed agitated. 'You're making a mistake,' she kept saying, as they marched her across the office towards the lobby and the lifts. 'This is a terrible misunderstanding.' She was breathing heavily and sweating. As she passed, I could see the way beads of moisture were making tracks from her hairline down to her jaw, melting her foundation. She looked right back at me but seemed unable to focus. It was as if we were locked away behind a screen, already lost to her.

'I have to go back upstairs and get my bag,' she wheezed.

'No need for that,' said Blue-Skirt, expressionlessly.

Elaine began to shake. 'I can't leave the building without my bag!' She tried to break free but they had her wedged between them and they kept moving her towards the lifts. 'You don't understand!' The suits clamped her all the more tightly. Elaine's feet paddled, her body twisting. 'I'm on medication. My medication is in my bag!'

'There'll be a doctor on duty where you're going,' the man said. 'You can talk to him about whatever it is you need.'

Elaine gave a despairing, almost animal howl. 'No, NO. I need my medication!'

They were out in the lobby by now. The lift doors pinged open and a pair of disembodied hands reached out to claim Elaine. 'Nooooo,' she wailed. The doors slid closed again and the noise stopped abruptly. It was as if Elaine had never even existed.

There was a frozen silence.

I was beginning to feel a bit ill, or possibly hungry. I wondered if I might be sickening for something. Perhaps I just needed the loo.

'Poor Elaine,' Roxanna whispered, blinking away tears.

'A disgrace,' muttered Derek. 'An absolute disgrace.'

People coughed and shifted uneasily. I could see that some weren't sure whether he meant Elaine, or what had been done to her.

Liz gave me a knowing look. 'No smoke without a fire, as they say.' A few of the more literal-minded people glanced up at the sprinkler system.

'Yeah, and what was all that business about "my medication"?' said Bob. 'You'd think she was an addict, the way she was going on.'

Roxanna said she'd heard that Elaine suffered from a chronic condition, some kind of wasting disease. She couldn't remember what. There were stifled giggles at the idea of an accountant with a *wasting* disease.

'Life is a wasting disease,' said Bob, waving a lobster-collared arm.

Liz and I exchanged a look that said: *idiot*.

Several people clearly preferred Bob's theory. Addicts were notoriously unreliable. They told lies – perhaps even lies about their health. They could be blackmailed. That would explain a lot. That would be a much more comfortable explanation.

'No,' said Roxanna. 'No, no, no!'

I was shifting from one foot to the other. 'I really need the loo,' I whispered to Liz.

'Leave it to me,' said Liz.

She went up and talked to the suits. Eventually, after Liz had employed the phrase 'Health and Safety', Blue-Skirt agreed to escort a small party of us to the ladies, which entailed going through to the offices on the other side of the lifts.

As we crossed the lobby, I considered making a dash for the stairs. I imagined myself running, making it all the way to the ground floor and then out into the street. The idea of outside sparked a sharp longing in my chest. I pictured light, fresh air, sky. But everything I needed was back in the other room: my bag, my keys, my money, my phone, my job. If I left now I might never be allowed back. And then what? Three hundred and fifty rejections. Think of that. My rebellious impulse withered.

'Come on then!' Blue-Skirt nodded for us to walk ahead of her, into the Admin and Human Resources section.

Here, too, there were men and women in suits conducting searches. Things seemed further advanced in this part of the building. They had made all the admin staff take off their shoes and kneel, barefoot, with their hands clasped behind their backs and their faces to the wall. I snatched furtive looks as we went by. I knew most of them – portly, argumentative, middle-aged women, every one of them silent now. I felt a strange muddle of emotions: surprise that tactics like this should be necessary; sadness for the women themselves, few of whom dared look around; and quite inexplicably a surge of guilt. But mostly, what I felt was relief that I myself was walking and not (yet) kneeling. In the current climate, that was something to be grateful for.

DEBTS

It was a Saturday. Martin was watching football on TV and Becky was in her room playing with her headless Barbies. In the kitchen, Kay put the letter from the debt collectors back behind the box of tin foil and stood for a while, watching an ant rush about on the worktop. It seemed to feel her finger coming. Perhaps she cast a shadow. Perhaps her finger made a noise as it came down, like a jet plane out of the sky. Whatever the reason, the ant knew it somehow and tried wildly to save itself: criss-crossing about on the imitation marble surface, pretending not to notice that it was about to die, its little whirring legs going like the clappers. Then her finger connected and it was over. The end.

'Kay?' Martin was calling from the front room. 'Kay, what are you doing out there?' She was meant to be bringing him a beer.

The doorbell went. 'I'll get it!' Martin yelled.

Kay glanced out from the kitchen. It was the odd-job boy, wanting to clean the car again. He would have cleaned it every day if Martin let him. He drove Kay wild, hanging about all the time. 'Ah, Kay,' Martin would say, 'he's just a poor lost boy who has nobody in the world.'

It seemed to Kay that if that boy was lost anywhere it was in a fog of stupidity. Once he came round asking for Martin in the middle of the week, and when she told him that Martin was at work, the boy had said: 'Well, is his wife in then?' 'I am his wife,' said Kay, and the boy said, 'Oh,' looking at her as if for the first time. 'I thought you was the nanny.'

'He imagines we're rich,' said Martin, laughing when she told him. 'He lives in a fantasy world. But what do you care?'

He was right of course. It was ridiculous to take the boy so seriously.

Today he was carrying a briefcase and had a flat cap set at a jaunty angle on his head. She could hear him droning on to Martin: 'Had a bit of business to take care of in the area, so I thought I'd call in here, like, just to see if ...'

Kay reached behind the tin foil and twitched out the letter once more:... *the sum of £3,387 due in settlement of rent arrears on the tenancy in your name in Water Street. Notify us of your arrangements to pay or we will begin court proceedings forthwith.* The page was headed with the name of a debt collection agency somewhere in the south-east. 'Vesta Holdings' it said at the top of the page, and a little cat lay curled in the lip of the V: hearth, home, heart – we repossess them all. How had they found her? Phone book, probably. The listing here was in her name. She hadn't been expecting trouble. She'd trusted Sue and Adam to keep paying the rent. She could hear Martin coming back down the hall to fetch a bucket of hot water for the boy. Becky followed along behind, trying to catch hold of his legs and shrieking with laughter.

'Let's go shopping, Daddy! For sweets.'

'Sweets!' came Martin's voice. 'You don't need sweets! If you got any sweeter you'd make us sick, my girl!'

Kay stuck the letter in the cutlery drawer, under some spoons and bits of string. She would tell him later; when things had quietened down.

The boy had been working on the car for about ten minutes and they were just sitting down to eat when the doorbell went again. Kay jumped up in a temper, thinking it would be the boy after another bucketful of water. But this time it was Wilson. Oh my, said Kay to herself, the tide really is flowing down our way today. Wilson stood there grinning at her, with a girl she'd never seen before beside him on the step.

'Hi there,' Kay said flatly. She was about to say that it wasn't really such a good time but Wilson got in first.

'We're meeting up with some people over in Clapham

later on so we thought we'd look in on you on the way.'

The girl stared at Kay intently. Wilson must have been talking about her beforehand, Kay thought. She could imagine Wilson building up a fantastically unrealistic portrait. ('My friend Kay.') She hoped they wouldn't be expected to have girlish chats in the kitchen about Wilson in his younger days. What could you say? He was the sort of person who couldn't button his shirts in the right order but could tell you about quantum physics if you had a few hours to spare.

'This is, um, Charity by the way,' Wilson said, 'Charity.' He made a little dip and a half turn towards the girl. His eyebrows danced a complicated apology. 'Her mother was a hippie.'

'She's a lawyer now,' the girl said quickly. 'She does a lot of property deals.'

'Well, that's OK then. Come inside!' Kay and Wilson laughed; Charity did not. Kay noticed that she had bad teeth and spoke as if she was always in a hurry to close her mouth, which made her look unfriendly. 'We were just having a late lunch, or maybe it's an early supper, I'm not too sure. We slept late today.'

'Brilliant,' Wilson said, rubbing his hands, always hungry.

Kay felt a flash of annoyance, but she suppressed it because things were still a bit uneven between her and Wilson. She had treated him badly once and he had taken it well, which left her on weak ground.

Martin got up from his meal and pulled the table away from the wall, found extra chairs and was welcoming. Becky stared until the newcomers were settled, then she stood up on her chair and shouted:

'I got red knickers on, I have.' She hiked her dress up over her drum-like stomach. 'Look!'

Everyone laughed.

Charity sat down beside Becky, folding her matchstick arms across her chest, and Kay went back into the kitchen for more plates. Wilson followed, loping behind her like a loose-limbed hound.

When she opened the drawer to get extra knives and forks she saw the letter curling out from under the spoons. She couldn't help herself.

'I had a letter this morning about the old flat. God almighty Wilson, it's so awful, I don't know what to do.'

Wilson dipped his head with a look of real concern, the way people look at sick animals or children woken by nightmares. 'What's the matter?' he murmured. 'What's wrong?'

'You know, the tenancy was always in my name, even though in the end I was sharing with Sue and Adam. Remember?'

It was terrible to be telling Wilson like this when she hadn't even told Martin yet, but Martin would panic. He was always entirely unprepared for trouble. He would say that she gloried in disaster, that her pessimism invited this kind of thing; he would accuse her of ruining his weekend. Wilson, on the other hand, was good on practical matters. He knew about gas and electricity and bureaucracy; he understood the laws of the little grids on which they lived. He might know what to do about this. He was nodding now, running a hand over his stubbly chin.

'When Martin and I moved out we looked into transferring the tenancy to them but it couldn't be done. No subletting. No transfers. So in the end I just left Sue with the rent book and sort of trusted them to keep on paying. But the place is still in my name.'

'Oh dear,' Wilson murmured. 'And they've skipped?'

Kay nodded. 'Disappeared. And the council has debt collectors chasing me for three grand's worth of unpaid rent, all in my name. Debt collectors! Can you believe it? Wilson?' Suddenly she wished she could go all floppy and burst into tears and have someone come over and make it all right again. She leaned against the sink. 'It's so awful I can't even think about it.'

Wilson half-lifted a hand as if to touch her shoulder, then seemed to think better of it. There was a long silence. Kay waited hopefully but all Wilson said was, 'Bad news, eh.'

'Here, take these plates,' Kay snapped, pretending to be suddenly busy.

'... it's the price of democracy, isn't it?' Charity was saying when they came back into the room. 'You have a community of bigots who want to elect a racist, and unless you're prepared to deny their political freedoms you have to allow it.' They were talking about the British National Party winning seats in local elections.

'Democracy is a grossly overrated concept,' Kay said, handing Charity her knife and fork.

'She used to be a Maoist,' Wilson said to Charity, writhing with delight.

'A mouse?!' Becky shrieked with amusement. 'Silly Wilson. A mouse is small, small, small like this,' she held up two fingers about an inch apart. 'And my mum is big nearly up to the roof. Look!'

Wilson nodded politely. He wasn't used to children. Becky gave another peal of loud social laughter and looked to Charity. 'Silly, isn't he, Chatty? Wilson is so silly!'

Charity ignored her.

'This isn't an academic question, Charity,' Martin continued over Becky's head. 'If this man gets elected in a borough with one of the biggest Bengali communities in London, then you legitimize the attacks, the talk of repatriation, the harassment ...'

'I know that,' said Charity calmly. 'That's why the bigots want him. It's a moral dilemma.'

Back in the kitchen again for the salt, Kay said, 'She looks very young, Wilson.'

'Twenty-four,' Wilson said. 'But that's not the problem. She's got a dead boyfriend. He speaks to her nearly every day.' Wilson rolled his eyes apologetically.

Kay wanted to laugh but she controlled herself. 'Is he

long dead?'

'Fell off a boat, six months ago off the coast of Africa. She never saw the body, which makes it worse apparently. And they parted on bad terms.'

'Poor Wilson. How can you compete?'

'It's difficult,' said Wilson, nodding. 'I can buy her a few drinks when I get my benefits. And there's sex, I suppose. But it's difficult. The dead have a strong hand.'

When they returned to the table Charity had moved on to talking about her sister. She and Martin seemed to be getting along extremely well. There were little pink spots on Charity's cheeks. She had hardly touched her food.

'... and she's involved with this awful man. I think ... well, I think he might be violent sometimes, I'm not really sure ...' Charity faltered.

Kay looked at her. Charity believes her sister is being knocked about, but she pretends she isn't sure because otherwise she'd have to do something about it. And she imagines that this way her conscience is clear. How amazing.

'Whatever,' Charity shrugged, 'he's really horrible. I don't know what she sees in him.'

'Chatty! Chatty! You know, Chatty?' Becky was insistent. 'Wilson is so silly! Ahhahahahaha! Do you smoke?'

Charity looked uncomfortable. 'No, I don't.'

Becky spooned food into her mouth, staring fixedly at Charity. Kay glanced over at Martin. She thought he was looking tired. If they'd been on their own he'd have been watching the football or sleeping now. He smiled at her. Out in the street, the odd-job boy had at last finished the car wash and stood back, admiring his work. After a moment, perhaps feeling himself observed, he leaned in and began furiously to apply the first coat of wax. Kay could almost hear the effort as he stretched over the bonnet, pushing at the cloth with all his weight. His briefcase stood on the pavement by the lamp post. His cap was stuffed into the back pocket of his jeans; the boy that nobody wanted.

'Perhaps it sounds uncaring,' Charity said, 'but I'm beginning to wonder whether some people don't just seek out relationships where they can be unhappy. I think people get addicted to pain. I can't see any other explanation for it, really.' She cut her lasagne into neat squares.

'Blame the victim, you mean?' Martin said.

Charity sat straighter in her chair and her eyes grew bright. It was hard to imagine her talking to a dead man.

'Is she a victim? Think about it for a minute. She's not exactly trapped. It's not as if she's got kids. It's not as if she hasn't got her own income.'

'I reckon it's a bit more complicated than that,' Kay said.

Wilson didn't look at her. 'It is,' he said slowly. 'It is much more complicated.'

'Some people do smoke Chatty, you know. Some people do smoke.'

'Leave Charity in peace for a minute now, Becky.'

'There is really no one to blame but herself because it's her choice, isn't it?' Charity leaned in and sparkled at Martin.

Kay didn't mind. There were always plenty of people who wanted to come and sparkle at Martin. Let them all come: the lost boys and girls, the ex-cons, the recovering junkies, the emotional cripples, they would find their way to him whether she liked it or not. It was as if there was a sign shining above his head saying: I am indestructible, dump it all here. The quality that sometimes irritated Kay – his groundless, almost childlike belief that things would inevitably come right in the end – was, to the people that sought him out, a gleam of loveliness in the dark.

'The fish is poorly again,' Kay turned to Wilson. 'I don't think it's fin rot after all. It seems to have lost its ability to float.'

Even after all this time they still had a habit of talking about domestic things: pets and plants and suchlike.

'The swim bladder could be blocked. Try putting it in

a bath of salt solution,' he said.

'Not while we're eating, please,' Martin muttered.

Becky started to loop her fork through her food and up to her mouth, faster and faster, so that bits of salad and peas and pasta shot out around the table. 'Lookatmeee, Chatty! Look at me eatin' fast! Hahahahahah!'

'Becky,' said Martin sternly, 'show Wilson and Charity how nicely you can eat.'

'NO!' yelled Becky. 'I got red knickers and I eat fast!' A piece of pasta flew off her fork and fell on Martin's sleeve.

'BECKY! Do you want to go to your room?'

Everyone stared at Martin. Even he seemed alarmed by the ferocity of his reaction but he organized his face into a stern glare. Becky sulked at her plate: 'No.'

'Well then, eat nicely.'

'I heard the other day,' said Wilson, 'that birds are beginning to imitate the sound of car alarms.'

'How depressing,' said Kay. 'Whatever for?'

Wilson was watching Charity; Martin was watching Becky.

'Because the sounds are there and fall within the range of what the birds will accept. But also because the birds want to fool their enemies into thinking they're bigger and more fearsome than they really are.'

'How sad,' said Kay.

'Sad?' said Charity. 'I think it's funny!'

Becky smiled a slitty-eyed, saccharine smile and stabbed an index finger in the middle of her plate.

'Beck-ky,' said Martin.

'Funny?' said Kay.

'Yes, funny,' said Charity. 'A starling pretending to be a car alarm. I think it's hilarious! Don't you?' she turned to Wilson.

Wilson looked uncomfortable.

Becky was smiling and tapping her fork in an unnaturally bright way.

26

'This is my food, this is my food,' she sang in an itty-bitty voice. 'This is my food, this is my food – and Eeeooooh! Now it's *gone!*' With a flick of her hand she sent the plate spinning up into the air. Charity didn't make a sound. Her mouth just fell open in surprise as she sat gazing at the crumpled sheets of lasagne in her lap. The plate slithered and bounced to the floor. Martin was on his feet.

'That's it!' he shouted, grabbing Becky by the arms. The child threw back her head and let out a piercing yell. 'I warned you, Becky. I warned you! You're a very naughty girl and you're going to your room!'

'No! No! No-OOO!'

Martin clamped her, kicking and struggling, against his chest. Kay could see that he was scared. He was shaking. He didn't know what else to do but go on with this because everybody was staring. 'Somebody has to draw the line around here!' he shouted. 'You're clearly not going to do anything. Someone's got to take responsibility!'

They heard the thud of his feet up the stairs, the slam of the bedroom door, then Becky screaming and pounding at it from inside, raging in disbelief. No one had ever done anything remotely like this to her before.

Charity got up and went to clean the lasagne off her jeans. Then she and Wilson gathered their things, watching Kay with solemn eyes. Kay walked them to the door and closed it behind them. She went into the kitchen and ran some water into the sink. Then she went upstairs. Martin and Becky were sitting on the landing, clasped in one another's arms.

'I'm sorry, Becky,' Martin was saying, over and over. 'I'm sorry, my sweetheart. I didn't mean it. I'm sorry.'

Becky had her face buried in his neck, hiccupping.

'Don't apologize,' Kay said. 'If you're going to do something like that, don't imagine you can take it back five minutes later.'

'Go away, Mummy,' Becky said, twisting her arms more tightly around Martin's neck, 'I don't want you,

Mummy. I want Daddy.'

Kay felt a little claw of dread. She thought about Charity and her sister and her freedom of choice. Was this how it began?

Then the bell rang: three loud bursts, restless and aggressive as a kick.

'It's that bloody boy again!' Kay shouted. 'I'm going to tell him to bugger off and leave us alone. I wish everybody would just leave us alone for once. Just for once!'

Martin came running after her down the stairs. 'Leave this to me, Kay! This has nothing to do with the boy. I don't want you taking it out on him.'

Becky was pulling on his legs and crying. They reached the front door together and wrenched it open, their faces hot and contorted with rage. There was the boy with his briefcase and cap.

'I've finished, Guv,' he said, looking serenely at Martin. 'I think you'll find I've done a lovely job.'

They all turned to look at the car – magnificently waxed and glittering in the road – and it began to rain. Great gouts of water fell out of the sky like eggs, bouncing and exploding on the dry ground. The boy's face crumpled in disbelief.

'Oh no,' he said softly. 'Look at that.'

Later, when Becky was asleep, Kay took the letter from the kitchen drawer and laid it on Martin's lap. Then she went out and sat on the covered porch at the back of the house. After about five minutes Martin came and joined her. He was remarkably calm.

'I wish you'd told me earlier,' he said.

'I was waiting for the right moment.'

'That would have been a long wait,' he said, laughing a little. Then he took her hand and squeezed it. 'Don't worry. We'll manage somehow.'

Kay extracted her hand. 'I'm not asking you to contribute. It's my problem fair and square. I just wanted you to know about it.'

They were all played out now, running on empty. They sat side by side, leaning against the wall, looking out at the garden. The rain had been heavy and now there was a clean smell of earth and night-scented stocks. Water spread on every surface, pooling in the sagging hollows of cement around the house, dripping from the roof like black honey. It seemed to Kay that they could feel Becky through the brick against their backs, breathing inside the house.

'It's a lot of money,' Martin said carefully. 'Do you have a plan?'

Kay shrugged. 'I'll find out who has the file in the council and go and cry on their desk or something. I'll say I did hand back the keys, and it's all a big mistake.'

'You mean lie?' Martin sounded shocked.

'Mmmm,' said Kay.

She found her eyes growing accustomed to the dark. She began to make out one or two details of the garden: a scribble of daisies at the end of the lawn, a single lily dripping over the rockery, the dark mass of evergreen leaves scratching against the fence. She thought about the fish with its blocked swim bladder at the bottom of the pond, and Becky with her arms around Martin's neck. She thought about Wilson and Charity and the drowned lover and the lost boy, and all the threads that connected her to the people she cared about, and beyond them to the ones she was indifferent to or didn't even know. She thought about the way we use people to fill in the pieces of ourselves that are weak or missing or to stand in for the things we fear, and what a precarious balance it is, how easily the threads are broken. And then she saw the snails.

There were masses of them. She could just make them out in the light reflected from the house, dark shapes with their wobbling horns, sailing out onto the drenched cement, creeping across the spilled silver sand from Becky's playbox, heading into the grass like ships, a dark Armada slipping on their bellies across the wet.

'Look.' She tugged at Martin's arm 'There's hundreds of them.'

It was as if the rain had turned the earth to a carpet of pulsing jelly. For a while they just sat and watched. It made Kay feel like shivering or bursting into tears for some reason. A snail carried with it all the ingredients of happiness, she thought: it was both male and female, both inside and out, always at home and on the road, owing nothing and no one. It laid its own slimy tracks, and headed out, half-blind, unhurrying, unafraid – just travelling, travelling, God knows where.

'Oh,' she whispered. 'Look.'

And all around them the darkness seemed to shudder, crowded with ghosts and insubstantial claims.

When he was still Head of Department, back in the days when Policy and Evaluation still existed as a department, Martin used to like to hold forth on the future of work. 'In the knowledge-based economy, we will ask people to work "smarter" not "harder",' he would say, 'and until this old place catches on, it's heading for oblivion.' The words he forgot to mention, Julianne thought afterwards, were 'cheaper' and 'younger'.

After the Organizational Restructuring, perhaps because of the speed at which the security guards helped him out of the building, Martin left much of his library on management theory behind. Julianne offered to share it with Bob but he wasn't interested, so Julianne took the books home and read them in the evenings while her mother watched TV. Julianne found their language reassuring, uplifting even. In future, they said, organizations would disaggregate into a complex mix of profit centres, franchises, small firms and sub-contractors. Companies would retain a small core of permanent employees but most of those in work could expect to function as 'portfolio people', delivering services to a range of clients. Command and control management would be a thing of the past. She and Bob, Julianne discovered, had already arrived in 'computopia'. How lovely, she thought.

It was true that, in the new era, their work was far cleaner. Most of the information they needed could be obtained by email and their reports were lodged in the same way. They did not have to waste time communicating with other members of their own department since there were none; and soon the names of other departments – 'Payroll', 'Press Office', 'Research and Development' – ceased to conjure up a muddle of names and faces. They got a lot more done.

But it was lonely down in the basement. Sometimes

Julianne would think about the old office on the fifth floor, and how she used to watch the sun turn the river pale as paper at the end of the day, the way the glass buildings seemed to burn. Where they were now the only window faced a blind wall and the sun seldom found its way into the room. The silence was punctuated at intervals by urgent liquid thunderings from the men's room on the floor above them, and through the wall behind her desk she could hear the crunch and grind of the lifts.

'I reckon we should approach them with a project,' Bob said after six months or so, when they'd begun to feel relatively safe again. 'We should offer to do a post-Restructuring audit; a kind of economic health check of the whole organization. Otherwise they'll just forget we exist.'

Julianne touched the acupressure point on her neck and considered him thoughtfully. He was a small, neat man several years younger than she was. He had broad hands with moonlike nails, big ears, tiny eyes and fine teeth. He wore his fox-brown hair in a neat brush cut and his colourful shirts (pumpkin, biscuit, slate) buttoned up to the top without a tie. He was good at his job, Julianne thought. He had a knack of skimming through pages and pages of data, then coming up with small but startling insights. She was not particularly interested in men – they were all much of a muchness, as her mother said – but there was something very pleasant about Bob.

'You go and talk to them,' he said. 'You've read all those fancy books, haven't you? You've got the lingo.'

After the meeting, Julianne found herself running back along one of the endless corridors on the fourteenth floor, her feet clattering wildly on the parquet. She couldn't move nearly fast enough. At the first vacant office, she went in and rang Bob's extension number.

'What's happened? What did they say? Where are you now?' Bob's voice sounded compressed, pared down to the essentials.

'I'm still up here on the fourteenth floor. Oh, I wish you could have seen their faces!' She slapped the flat of her hand against her thigh. 'If we play this right, we can have them eating out of our hands!'

'Is the meeting finished?'

'You can't see any of this, can you?' She stopped and looked around her. She could see the river again: today it was choppy and almost black. 'It's quite extraordinary from up here. I'm in an empty office, just looking out, and oh my ...' Julianne laughed. She felt a kind of slow uncoiling of something in her veins.

She had always found it easier to talk on the phone. You didn't have to worry about arranging your body appropriately or how your face was behaving or where the other person's eyes were straying. You didn't have to worry about whether your breath smelled, or whether theirs did, or about any unwelcome invasions of your personal space. She settled herself on the empty desk. Her breathing slowed. She smiled, touched a hand to her neck again, and heard the rustle of her hair.

'What can you see?'

'There's a storm brewing,' she said. 'At the moment there's just the wind but the light is changing very fast and I think there's rain on the way. There are clouds coming in. Fat, purple clouds, and all the time the wind is stirring up the sky. There's bits of paper and leaves and birds being blown backwards. Everything is whipping about in the air. Everything is inside out and all over the place.'

There was a silence.

'You know what I'd like to do now?'

Still this crowded quiet on the line. She could hear his surprise and unease and excitement all coiled up together in the tightness of the optic fibre. 'What ...' He cleared his throat. 'What would you like to do?'

She laughed. 'I'd like to open the window and step right out into the middle of it all.'

33

'Don't do that,' he said quickly.

'I'm only talking,' she laughed. 'Stupid.'

When she got back to her desk she could feel him watching her but he said nothing about the phone call; nor did she. They started planning the audit project together as if nothing had happened. This must be what the books meant, thought Julianne, about manufacturing trust.

They designed and circulated detailed questionnaires to every department. They constructed a database and a statistical model, they broke the results of the questionnaire into inputs and outputs. It took them almost exactly a year. During that time, Bob and his wife increased the size of their mortgage and moved from a flat to a house; took package holidays in Greece and the Canary Islands; and talked vaguely about having a baby but agreed they weren't quite ready. Bob had twenty-five haircuts (all the same), and visited his dentist once for a minor filling. He turned twenty-seven on the day they completed the last of the data entries.

Julianne took no exotic holidays, preferring to spread her leave across a series of short visits to friends (since her mother didn't like her to be away for long), but she did think about moving. She was nearly thirty and she longed now for a place of her own. She got as far as contacting estate agents before her mother's angina flared up again. Julianne had ten haircuts during this time (changing the style twice), eight sessions in a flotation tank, twelve Chinese massages to release stress and three visits to an osteopath about a stabbing pain in her neck (her teeth were perfect). If these appointments fell during working hours, she would always ring the office.

After a while she began to ring on other days too. Not carelessly, by any means. She rationed herself. She'd make herself wait until she couldn't bear to wait any longer. Then she'd run back up to the empty room on the fourteenth floor. 'It's me,' she'd say. And Bob would reply, 'I was wondering when I was going to hear from you again,' as if she was another person entirely. She loved that. Five minutes later she'd be back behind her desk and they'd both behave as if nothing had passed between them.

The picture that emerged from their analysis of the questionnaires was clear. They could see that, even after the Restructuring, whole overweight subsections and divisions remained hanging on the organization like ticks on a dog, sucking up money and time. The animal must be shaved right back to the bone, then they would see it move, sleek and lean and full of hurt, going in for the kill.

'This is going to blow their socks off,' Bob would mutter to himself as he worked on his section of the report. But Julianne was less satisfied; she felt there was something missing. At home she was irritable and distant with her mother, only happy when she could retire to her room and read her management theory books. Work, said the books, should be reconceptualised as a pool that you moved to the centre of rather than a pyramid that you climbed. The aristocracy of the labour market would be the 'symbolic analysts' (consultants, planners, advertising executives).

Julianne began to have dreams at night where she saw herself walking down long corridors with jigsaw-like chunks of her body missing. Or she would be back on the fourteenth floor, and the head of personnel would say, 'We'll wait another minute or so for Ms Stack and then I'm afraid we'll have to begin,' and it would come to Julianne in a horrifying flash that they couldn't see her because she had been disaggregated, atomized, deleted.

By day Julianne wrote and rewrote her section of the report, delaying the very last sentence for as long as she could. She thought of Martin's books. When you found yourself in a blind alley, they said, it was best to turn your back on the problem and do something entirely different: swim, climb a mountain, dive from a plane – then, nine times out of ten, the solution would come to you like an apple dropping into your hand. She'd switch off her computer, then, and run up to the fourteenth floor: 'It's me. Did you miss me?'

'Of course. Tell me what you see?'

'Today? Oh, today the river is the colour of ...' Bananas, steam trains, the old Rover my Dad used to drive – she could sit up here and tell him anything and he would have to believe her. As she talked, she felt perfectly light and safe, and all her worries would be suspended by the limits of the line. But she knew also how tenuous it was, how easily it could be interrupted.

Bob tried calling her once. He must have gone out to a payphone because she could hear the swish of traffic in the background. His voice sounded harsh and grating in her ear.

'I dream about you, you know,' he said. 'I dreamed about you last night. Is it the same for you ...?'

Panic rolled under Julianne's skin: all the way up her back and over the top of her head. She nearly threw down the receiver but she made herself count to ten. From the floor above came the melancholy rush of water in the pipes.

With great effort she kept her voice steady. 'You don't understand this, do you Bob? You're trying to force the pace, hurry us along to the punchline. But what if there isn't one?' There was one of those dense, struggling silences on the line. 'You have to stop thinking in terms of ladders and pyramids and getting to the point. Think of this as a pool. Enjoy the moment. Swim, Bob, stop trying to climb.' She could hear him drowning out there, wherever he was. 'I'm hanging up now, OK?'

Later she went up to central admin support and got them each a tiny matt-black mobile by way of compensation. 'In case of an emergency,' she said. 'We should be able to contact one another.'

'What's your number?'

She saw how he couldn't quite meet her eye, how his pen trembled above the page of his jotter. 'No need for that,' she said. 'I'll make the calls.'

'Oh.' He set down his pen.

She slipped her mobile into her shoulder bag, slung over one hip; he dropped his into the breast pocket of his jacket, watching her. She could see he still didn't get it.

'It has to be me calling or it doesn't work,' she said. 'OK? I have to be in control.'

The next time Julianne stepped out of the lift on the fourteenth floor, she found everything swathed in dust sheets and the air heady with the smell of paint. Workmen in overalls were busy packing up for the day, stacking ladders and trestles against the walls, dumping rollers in tubs, sealing up big industrial containers of paint.

'What's going on?' she asked a man who stood wiping his hands on a paint-soaked rag. The smell of turps spread around him like an itch.

'Don't know, love,' he grinned. 'We've got a contract to redecorate the whole of this floor. Maybe they're renting it out? Who knows. They never tell us what they want it for.'

Julianne walked down the main corridor with offices peeling off on either side. She stopped at the door to the boardroom where she'd pitched their audit idea more than a year earlier. It was like all the rest now: clean, featureless, gleaming white. She could almost feel the next wave of occupants piling up behind her, impatient to move in and make their mark. What work would they do here? Management consultancy, political lobbying, PR – jobs that left no residue, jobs you didn't have to wash up after at the end of the day.

From the lifts she heard faint clangs and shouts, then silence as the workmen left the floor. She walked on to the little box room at the end of the corridor. There was a single hinged window looking out on the roof of the next building a couple of feet away. Julianne opened the window, leaning out as far as she dared to catch a splintered glimpse of the street.

Sometimes she toyed with the idea of applying for a job in a smaller place where she could be near the countryside and breathe fresh air. Her mother would go all pale and trembling when she talked like that. 'You always were like your father,' she'd say. 'Go on then. Go on. Walk away and leave me like this. I managed once, I suppose I'll manage again.' Julianne knew she would never do it. It wasn't just guilt; it was her love of the city itself. She liked the buzz, the anonymity, the competitive edge. If she put her mind to it, if they made a success of this report, there would be opportunities to move to a better job, something one or two ripples closer to the centre. She wouldn't really be satisfied with anything less now.

She reached into her little bag for the phone. 'Bob,' she said. 'Come up here a minute would you. I want to try out something. The fourteenth floor. Hurry.'

They took two great, solid planks from one of the painters' trestle tables and in no time at all they had built a bridge from the window where they stood to the roof of the opposite building.

Bob grinned: 'Now what?'

'I want you to walk across.'

Bob's face turned chalky with surprise. He looked from her to the window and back. 'Why would I do that?'

'How long have we been working on this report, Bob?'

'A year.'

'A whole year we've been buried down in that airless, lightless, underground box of an office and you know what, Bob? We've gone stale. We've lost our focus.'

'What's that got to do with me going out on that plank?'

'Sometimes, when you're working really hard you go sort of blind, Bob. You lose your sense of perspective and you need to stop and walk away from whatever it is you're doing. Sometimes it helps to do something apparently pointless: hot-air ballooning, abseiling. Take a few risks and suddenly you see things from a different angle. I swear, that's what the books say.'

Bob stared at her for a long moment. Then he reached into his jacket pocket for the little phone, clasping and unclasping it in the palm of his hand. 'I'll do it if I can make one call.'

Julianne felt her throat constrict but it was a fair trade-off: one fear for another. She nodded. Bob took off his jacket, then knelt and checked his shoelaces, hitching up his trousers so that they wouldn't get creased. Over by the window he stepped onto an upturned paint container, grabbed the window frame and hauled himself up onto the ledge. He crouched there for a long while, one foot on the planks, the other foot curled over the firm lip of the sill, both hands gripping the window frame.

'Go on Bob,' Julianne whispered, 'you can do it.'

He stood up, still holding onto the window frame but ducking his head out beyond it, keeping his knees still slightly bent. He edged his foot out a little way onto the planks, turning his body towards the open window. His shirt brushed the glass, his fingers clung and crawled along its metal ridge, his left foot slid further out onto the boards, till there was nothing but air beneath the wood. Slowly, slowly, still gripping the window frame with one arm, he pulled his body round till he faced the opposite building and his back was to Julianne.

She was struck suddenly by the frail physical fact of him. This is Bob, she thought, a bundle of flesh and blood and brain, a mass of raw human potential: flexible; suggestible; young; cheap; perfect.

'Go on Bob,' she whispered.

He slid his right foot up to meet the left, his fingers came clasp-clasping to the end of the window and fixed on the right angle, holding it like the knob of a cane. Julianne couldn't move, not even to suck breath into her lungs. She couldn't blink. She knew that if her eyes let him go, if she stopped concentrating even for a moment, everything would be lost. She was reduced to nothing but this moment, this place, this body in front of her. He muttered something but the wind carried it off. His left foot edged forward, then he let go of the window and edged out of its reach. This is what it's all about, she thought.

'You can do this Bob.'

Suddenly he was crouching in the middle of the bridge. He wobbled, then righted himself. 'Oh Jesus!' he shouted. 'Oh help me God!' but he was laughing at the same time.

Julianne frowned. What was he doing? He lurched, then righted himself, all the while fumbling for something in his shirt pocket. Another off-centre swoop and both arms flew out on either side of him. She saw the mobile in one hand. He brought his arms in again very slowly. After a moment the phone rang at her hip.

'Hullo?'

She closed her eyes and imagined him out there, in the middle of nowhere: thin as a toothpick, air swirling round his ears. 'Bob,' she said. 'You're doing really well, but don't lose your focus. Keep looking over at the far side and try –'

He cut her short. 'This is my call, Julianne. I talk and you listen this time, OK?'

Julianne was silent.

'OK?' he said again. He took a big breath. 'This time I am going to let it all out: all those things that crawl around in my brain night and day and drive me crazy. Sometimes I think that everything I'm not allowed to say to you is collecting up in a huge ball of mucus in my throat and that one day it's going to choke me right there at my desk. Sometimes I think … no, I'll start with the dreams, sometimes, Julianne, I … whooo! … Christ! What a rush this is. What a high!' He started laughing wildly. Julianne held the phone away from her ear. 'A shagging great fourteen-storey high!' he yelled. 'What a feeling. What an incredible feeling!'

Julianne looked out at the little figure teetering in the dirty afternoon air. She spoke softly into the phone again.

'Bob. This is serious. You must calm down. Concentrate. Otherwise you'll fall.'

'I swear, I'll never be afraid of anything in my life again, Julianne. Oh baby, when I get back in there I won't need a phone to say the things I want to say to you. No! It's going to be different from now on, sweetheart. I am not going to put up with ... Tell me something, did you try this stuff on Martin? Is that why they sacked him? Or am I losing my sense of perspective? What the hell. What difference does it make? Let me tell you about my dreams. In my dream you're in this short green skirt and you're standing on a ladder just behind my desk and I know that if I turn my head ...'

Julianne stopped listening at this point. She had a sudden flash of insight, just as the books said she would. She understood three things: (1) that Bob did not perform well under pressure; (2) that she was looking at an image of the future, that this was the way their children and their children's children would work, without nets or props, nerveless and weightless and up against the wire; and (3) that her next job would be in some kind of management capacity.

'... and you're wearing this really thin shirt and ... whoo!'

Julianne looked out of the window in time to see him lurch again. Both his arms flew out to right his balance, but this time the mobile phone kept going. Julianne followed its trajectory through the air: a high, sweet arc which was quite irresistible to the eye. Only when the phone peaked and began to plummet, did Julianne look back at the plank.

For a moment she didn't move. Then she lifted a hand to caress the acupressure point on her neck. 'Oh dear,' she murmured.

MISTAKEN

Arlette pushed through the heavy glass doors of the London department store and into the blaze of light that was Cosmetics. She was looking for a birthday present for her sister, but it was hard to concentrate. Her mind was on work and the speech the Dean had made earlier that week: *Changing demographics; Economic downturn; 80 per cent cuts in teaching budgets; 100 per cent cuts to Humanities' research. This university is going to have to innovate if it's going to survive. That was the gist of his end of term message: Innovate or ...*

Arlette brushed past a girl in a lab coat who was rolling her hands in a bowl of glycerine flecked with gold. Two middle-aged women stood listening humbly to her sales chatter: '... collagen repairs and revitalizes ... brightens and exfoliates ... luxurious ... scientifically proven ... space-age technology ...'

You have an opportunity to reinvent yourselves with this current curriculum review, the Dean had said. *You're all intelligent, creative people. I have every confidence ...*

Arlette stepped onto the escalator and rose up into Handbags and Accessories, cursing herself. She should have seen this coming. Why had she not been more proactive? She'd been languishing on a 0.4 contract for several years, hoping that a proper job would open up, and now look. That morning, her line manager, Hamish, had called her in for a meeting which began with: 'In the current climate'. He'd gone on to say a lot of other things such as: '... shared modules ... cross-funding ... inter-departmental collaborations ... focus on recruitment and retention ...' – tugging miserably at the diamond stud in his ear. They could reduce her hours if her modules didn't recruit so she would have to be 'super' flexible about class sizes and 'Perhaps we need a fresh approach? Courses our competitors haven't thought of? Modules we can flog

43

to other degrees?' Arlette knew what he wanted. Sexy, buzzy titles to keep student numbers up. Bums on seats. *Luxurious. Scientifically proven. Space-age technology. You're all intelligent, creative people.* Damn, damn, damn. She didn't even want to think about it.

She paused in Womenswear to finger a pretty silver party dress. There was something about it that swept away all the stresses of the day and pitched her back to the feeling of being sixteen again: knowing nothing and wanting everything, burning with longings, dreaming of the life she was going to lead as soon as she could escape suburbia and her mother's 10 p.m. curfew. It was the colour, she decided, that particularly luminous shade of ice-blue. It reminded her of the sea in Géricault's *Raft of the Medusa.* At sixteen, when she was supposed to be studying, she used to spend hours leafing through the art books in the library, fingering the shiny colour plates; the Géricault had been her favourite. Part of its power lay in the fact that she knew it depicted a real shipwreck: that the captain and crew had taken to the lifeboats and these poor wretches on the raft had expected to be towed to safety but instead were cut loose with almost no supplies; only the centre of the raft was safe; the kegs of water they'd been given fell into the sea and only wine remained; the weak and dying were kicked overboard and people ate the flesh of the already dead because there was no food. She liked the fact that it was a black man at the apex of the pyramid of bodies. He had his back to the viewer, waving at some invisible rescuer on the skyline. Take me away, take me away from here.

Arlette returned her attention to the dress, stroking the silver fabric with an open palm. Shipwreck chic. You had to be young to carry it off. Well, she wasn't exactly old – not yet. Her spirits lifted. *Innovate, Arlette. Be creative!*

She forgot all about her sister's present. She dropped her bag and coat in a quiet corner and stepped up to a mirror holding the dress under her chin, squinting. Too

44

tinselly. She put it back and picked out another style. No again. Too badly made. But now she was hooked on the idea of buying herself a dress. As her fingers skipped through the hangers on the rail she was vaguely aware of a noise at the edge of her attention, a voice calling, 'Excuse me!' *Innovate. Be creative.* Blue? Yellow? Cerise? She couldn't really blame Hamish. He had people digging pins into him from above. The message was clear, though. If she wanted to hang on to her job she must cobble together some up-to-the-minute-sounding outlines that Hamish could go off and sell to both senior management and students. It stuck in her craw to do it, but the alternative was probably unemployment, which her mother had been predicting for years.

She flicked more roughly through the ranks of cloth. Stripes. Flowers. Lace-effect. No to all that.

'EXCUSE me! Hul-LO!' The voice was getting louder and more furious, 'EXCU-USE ME!!!'

At last Arlette had to turn. She saw a smartly dressed white woman and a girl of about twelve standing at one of the unattended cash desks. 'We'd like to PAY for this, IF you don't mind!'

For a brief out-of-body moment Arlette saw herself as she must appear to this woman: a thirty-something black woman rearranging the stock. Staff. Help. Service. (*You have an opportunity to re-invent yourself, Arlette ...*)

'... IF that's not too much trouble for you ...' the woman hissed.

Arlette blinked. How swiftly a woman like this could strip her of all her accomplishments: her grade 5 piano (with Distinction), her ballet lessons, her carefully modulated accent, her fistful of A* grades, her doctorate – gone, all gone in an instant. She opened her mouth to speak. But what could she say? I'm not a shop assistant, I'm a ... what? Not a Professor, nor a Reader. Not a HoD or a Chair. Not a mother, nor a wife, nor even properly the author of anything, not recently anyway. A great fury rose within her like an underwater wave, lifting her like a toy on the lip of a tsunami. She moved over to the cash desk, took the skimpy top they wanted, flipped it, folded it, slipped it into a bag from the pile under the counter and the woman handed over a credit card. It was beautifully easy. It flowed.

'Just a moment,' Arlette murmured in a silky tone. 'I need to get authorization.'

She spoke with such confidence that the woman seemed briefly hypnotized. One of the lifts opened as if by magic as she approached. She held the card between thumb and forefinger like an after-dinner mint, stepped inside, turned and blew the pair of them a little kiss. The woman gave a howl of outrage. 'My card!!' Then the lift doors closed and the computerized voice said: 'Going UP!' and Arlette was whisked away, laughing.

'Can I help you?' A young shop assistant peered in at her through the curtains of the changing cubicle.

Arlette wasn't laughing any more. Even the six items she'd wrenched from the rail outside didn't justify the time she'd been lurking here.

'Could you get me all of these in a larger size, please?'

The girl took the jumble of clothing and glanced thoughtfully at the labels. She looked back at Arlette. 'If there is something else you need you can tell me. Is OK.' She was a pale blonde girl, slim and upright; eastern European, judging by the accent.

Arlette was tempted to say something snappish and haughty, but they were interrupted by a loud crackling from a walkie-talkie somewhere outside the cubicles and a man's voice calling, 'Hullo? Who's in charge here?'

The girl disappeared.

Arlette slumped back down on the bench. The place was crawling with in-store security. The bank card would be discovered sooner or later on the unattended cash desk where she'd dropped it, but they'd probably snagged an image of her before that on CCTV. It was only a matter of time before they tracked her down, and then what was she going to say? I took it by mistake? I mis-took it? I was mistaken? *She* was mistaken? She took me for a shop girl so I took her for a ride? How could she have been so stupid, risking so much for a brief giddy moment of satisfaction? Her sister would never have been caught like this.

The girl returned. 'A woman has stolen a credit card,' she said. 'They think she is still somewhere in the building.'

Arlette set her jaw and glared out into the middle distance. She couldn't bring herself to grovel. In her mind, she had her back turned and she was waving, waving at the horizon. Save me. Save me. I am destined for something other than this.

'They wanted to come to search in here, but I said I did not see ... anyone like they described.'

'Meaning what exactly?'

The girl just looked at her.

Arlette sighed. 'OK. OK. What do you want me to do?'

'Right now they are watching all exits, but I can take you to a place where you can wait until it is safer. I know how to walk so that the cameras do not see. I can walk through whole shop and not be seen. I can show you.'

'Why would you do that? You don't even know me.'

'You want that I help you?' said the girl. 'For me is all the same.'

Time passed slowly in the stockroom. Arlette sat on a pile of boxes right at the very back where, as the girl had said, no one came. She closed her eyes and folded her hands in her lap, and gave herself up to the faraway fluttering noises of the shop. Footsteps. Voices. Rustling bags. The distant, tinny ping of the lifts. Ship-wrecked. Shop-wrecked.

She thought about Hamish in his vintage Malcolm McLaren bondage trousers and the Dean in his businessman's suit. She thought about the university's corporate plan and their 'direct competitors', and all the

47

rest of the people working in post-'92 universities, and beyond that the Redbrick and the Plate-glass universities, and the Russell group. She saw all of them as figures in Géricault's tableau: cast adrift by an incompetent Royalist captain, struggling and elbowing one another to get to the safest point at the centre, tearing into the flesh of the dead to survive.

Funny that after all this time she should be thinking about Géricault again. She could imagine Hamish's expression of distaste – Realist painting? Ugh! But perhaps she could write a little piece about it for *Art Quarterly*: the significance of the black man waving; painting as reportage; voyeurism; scopophilia; cannibalism. She got to her feet in a confused rush of feeling until she remembered where she was. No point in running out and getting arrested.

At around six the blonde girl returned and stood beckoning her from the far side of the stockroom. 'Pssst! Now is good. They have much trouble with teenagers in Phones and Hi-fi. Everyone very busy.'

Somehow she had managed to find Arlette's coat and bag. She stifled all expressions of gratitude with a brusque: 'It was where you said: first floor, in corner. Put it on. They are not looking for a woman in coat.'

They cut through the middle of Home Furnishings – 'Walk exactly behind me and we will not be seen' – circumnavigated Fitness and Camping, slid along the very edge of Haberdashery and out through the doors marked EXIT to the echoing back staircase. No one gave them a second glance.

On the last step of the last flight, when the doors to the street were in sight, the blonde girl paused and touched Arlette on the arm. 'Put your collar up. Like so. Go through the door and turn right. Do not stop walking until you are away from here and you will be OK.'

'You've been so kind,' said Arlette. 'Thank you.' And then, although it was far too late and she knew it was foolish, she began to try and explain to the girl about the card. 'I left it on one of the counters. I wasn't trying to steal it, but she was just so rude and ...'

'Is OK,' said the girl, waving a hand. 'You don't need to tell me anything. You are like my sister.'

Arlette almost laughed aloud. Such a corny line, and so unexpected from a stony-faced blonde like this. Sisters under the skin. All God's children. We all bleed the same colour blood, etc. Ten years ago, when she still had the poster of Angela Davis above her bed, a simple-minded statement like this would have driven her wild, but now she only murmured, 'That's so sweet of you.'

'My sister, too, is a klepto,' the girl continued. 'I understand. Is disease, not crime.'

Arlette felt the blood rush to her cheeks. 'No, no, I ...!' The girl just nodded and turned away and began to climb the stairs again, back to Womenswear.

Arlette watched her go. Oh. She was mistaken. They are mistaken. We were mistaken. Oh. And then she laughed and turned her back on the shop and began to walk, and soon she too was gone from there, lost in the flow of shoppers, waving, waving at the horizon.

'Is this Mrs McClusky's house?' The speaker – a stout, blond child of about ten – stood on the other side of the gate.

Eric straightened up and leaned on his spade, enjoying the feel of the metal as it sank into the well-tended soil.

'Depends.' He grinned. 'Who's asking?'

The boy frowned. 'Mrs McClusky goes to our church.'

'Does she now?'

Eric had been doing Mrs M's garden for about three years, ever since the Croydon business. He tended to say 'early retirement' when he talked about all that. As in: 'I used to be a night-watchman but then I had to take early retirement'. Mrs M was also retired. She'd been a head teacher, which probably meant she had a big fat pension. She had a metal grille over her front door, which she kept locked unless she was coming out to bring Eric tea and biscuits. She usually did that in the afternoon around four o'clock.

'My name is Thomas,' said the child. 'Mrs McClusky is expecting me.'

'I used to know a Thomas,' Eric said. 'In the children's home. Big lad. Handy with his fists.'

'That must be a different person,' said the boy. 'I do not live in a children's home. I live with my mother and my mother's boyfriend.'

'I see,' Eric muttered, although he didn't at all, in fact he closed his eyes for a second or two. He hadn't been feeling too well lately.

'Mrs McClusky.' The boy's tone grew insistent. 'Do you know if she is in the house?'

Only now did Eric notice that the lad had a bit of an accent: howz, he said. Oh-ho! This gave him some ammunition. 'You're not English, are you? Where are you from?'

This seemed to resolve things for the boy. He stopped making eye contact. He lifted the latch, opened the gate and walked up the path to the house as if Eric had ceased to exist.

'Kosovo, is it?' Eric called after him. 'Croatia? Romania? How about Bulgaria?'

The boy ignored him and rang the doorbell.

'Czech Republic? Serbia? Poland?' That produced a brief, flickering glance. 'Ah-ha! Gotcha! You're Polish. Aha-ha-hah! I knew it!'

'If you were in a quiz you would get not-any-points for that,' the boy said coldly. 'You have to know the answer first time. Guessing is not the same as knowledge.'

Eric rested back on his spade again, winded by the cheek of the lad. 'Little beggar,' he muttered. He repeated the phrase more loudly for Mrs M's benefit when she appeared at the door. She paid no attention. She unlocked the grille and, smiling, ushered the boy inside. Oh-ho! Like that, is it? thought Eric. This smarty-pants foreign boy was invited into the house, but he, Eric, was only good enough for the garden? So that's how the land lay. Now it was out in the open.

He turned back to his digging: rooting, twisting, stabbing at the earth with the spade. He tore up a clump of couch grass. He massacred a bramble, then turned on the stump of dead forsythia that had been mouldering in a corner all the time he'd been working for Mrs M: three years, and never once in all that time had he been invited to cross that threshold.

After about half an hour, young Bobby passed by on the road carrying a small dog under one arm. 'Hiya, Eric.'

Eric straightened up and nodded.

Bobby was eighteen years old, pale, spotty, always hunched over to one side, a bit wrong-looking. People said it was because Bobby's mother had been drunk all the time when she was carrying him. But at least Bobby had a mother. He knew the sound of her voice and where she

52

could be found at any time of the day (at her cleaning job or in the pub). And he had a father, which was more than a lot of people could say. Bobby's father was a prison guard, a good job.

Eric told Bobby about the hoity-toity Polish boy. 'It's her I'm worried about. Lord knows what he's getting up to when her back is turned.'

Bobby nodded and waggled his eyebrows.

The dog gave a squeaky yawn.

''S my mum's,' said Bobby, by way of an explanation. 'It only walks when it knows it's going home so I've got to carry it off a ways, then put it down and it runs back. Otherwise it don't get no exercise.'

Eric laughed long and hard at that. You could always rely on Bobby for entertainment.

Bobby looked annoyed. ''S not my fault! It's a lady's dog.'

Mrs M and the Polish boy came out of the house now, and began to amble down the path, both of them smiling. Bobby hurried off. Eric redoubled his attack on the forsythia.

As Mrs M and the boy approached, Eric gave one last shoulder-wrenching tug and the root came loose, sending out a spray of earth and grit. Eric tossed the stump into the wheelbarrow where it landed with a satisfying clang. He clapped the soil from his hands.

'There!'

Mrs M beamed. 'Good work.' She put an arm around the boy's shoulders. 'We'll be seeing a fair bit of this young gentleman over the summer, Eric. Thomas will be coming to me once a week for some extra lessons.'

'Behind is he?' Eric's mood began to lift. 'Needs to brush up on his English, I expect.'

Not at all, said Mrs M. In fact, quite the contrary. Thomas was an exceedingly gifted child. She was going to be preparing him to sit the grammar school entrance tests in September.

'So that I don't have to go to the bad schools in this area,' the boy said in his high, unbroken voice, 'and be stabbed in my stomach with a kitchen knife.'

Mrs M laughed. 'Goodness me, Thomas! Where did you get that idea from?' And then, 'Don't dig on the left there, Eric. That's where the daffodil bulbs are. You said it wasn't worth lifting them. Remember?'

That didn't help his mood. Not at all.

It was a beautiful summer that year, hot and bright, with clear blue skies in the day and now and then a bit of rain at night. Good growing weather. Eric dug up the daffs and stored them in the shed so that he didn't have to put up with 'no-go zones'. Then he got rid of the choisya that had been blighted by the winter frosts and filled the gap with a mature weigela that Mrs M brought back from the garden centre together with trays of lobelia and pansies for the borders; she was extravagant like that, Mrs M.

The poppies and day lilies and white shasta daisies came up like fireworks, and when they were done Eric cut them back so that the stocks and delphiniums and hollyhocks could take over. The yarrow and echinacea made a steady show in the sunny bed at the front of the house, and on the other side the hostas and hellebores and sedge grass prospered stubbornly in the shade. Eric chopped them back whenever Mrs M wasn't looking, especially the hellebores.

He'd come late to an appreciation of nature, not having spent much time in places where things could grow. In the aftermath of the Croydon affair he thought for a while that he'd never work again. He had his army pension and some savings, but it wasn't enough. He sat around in his flat for weeks on end, nursing his injuries and brooding on the injustice of it all. The warehouse supervisor had said he should count himself lucky they were just letting him go instead of making it a matter for the police. Lucky?! A head injury and no job. No references. No compensation. A funny kind of luck.

After about a month, when the worst of the bruises had healed, he'd started going out to pubs and talking to whoever was willing to listen. 'I'm out on my ear and they've got some big fat Ruski doing my job, so explain to me how that's lucky? I'm still waiting to understand that. If I'd been the inside man, do you think I'd have let them hit me like that? Do you think I'd be sitting here talking to you now? I'd be living it up on the Costa del Sol. Wouldn't I?'

Eventually he met Stu and after that things began to look up. Stu was tough, loud and sinewy. He wore plaid shirts and steel-toed boots and he could beat anyone at arm-wrestling. He had an electric lawnmower, a chainsaw and a pickup truck. In summer he cut people's lawns, in the winter he did pest control and tree surgery. People were always asking Stu to do jobs that he didn't really have time for and he began to pass on the simple ones to Eric. One day, as Eric was trimming a hedge, Mrs M walked by and mistook him for a gardener. Before he knew it he'd built up a list of more or less regular clients and he was back on his feet again.

After a while, when he felt he knew her, he told Mrs M about the Croydon business. She was very sympathetic.

A lot of what Eric knew about gardening he'd learned from Stu. You had to keep an eye out for dandelions, bramble, burdock, ragwort, chickweed, bindweed, hogweed and ground elder. 'If you see any of that stuff, stamp it out,' said Stu. 'Fast.' The worst was Japanese knotweed, which was classed as an infestation. 'They set up an exclusion zone if they find it in a garden,' said Stu. It all reminded Eric a bit of the army.

'That's because life is a war,' said Stu. 'Kill or be killed. Eat or be eaten.'

Eradicate: that was Stu's favourite word.

All through the summer the Polish boy came for his lessons. He, too, was growing. Every week he looked as if he'd been inflated just a little more: longer arms, longer legs, a chunkier body, a less childish face. For a while there were big gaps between the ends of his sleeves and his wrists and between the ends of his trousers and his feet. Then someone must have taken him shopping because things fitted him again. Lucky beggar.

Sometimes, when he knew the boy was having his lesson, Eric would go round to the back of the house and snip away at the rose bushes so that he could see what they were getting up to in the house. They always sat at the dining-room table. The boy would be hunched over some bit of paper, scribbling, while Mrs M read over other work. On the table there'd be a cup of tea for Mrs M and a glass of juice for the boy, and always a big plate of biscuits. Sometimes Eric could get close enough to identify the type of biscuits: usually chocolate digestives, sometimes bourbons or custard creams; one week he saw the glint of something foil-wrapped. He had never been offered anything other than rich tea or plain digestives.

If it was hot they'd have the patio door open. Once, Eric heard Mrs M tell the boy that he had a wonderful imagination. Another time she said he had 'a real gift for algebra'. When she was particularly pleased, she would pat him on the shoulder. Eric couldn't remember ever being patted like that as a child. After he left foster care and went into the children's home nobody touched him at all, unless it was to straighten his clothing or to check his hair for lice. If there was ever a rumpus in the school yard he'd throw himself into the middle of it, just for the heart-thump of a body against his. It all got a bit muddled up in his head: connecting with other people and being pounded.

When he first got to know Stu he ended up going back to Stu's place quite a few times. They'd be drunk when they left the pub and then they'd drink some more and Stu would want to fight – arm-wrestling to begin with, then boxing, and somehow they'd end up in a tangle in Stu's bed, skin to skin. Once Eric was back on track again workwise he got tired of being covered in bruises so that side of their relationship tailed off. If Stu had ever said: You have a great imagination, Eric – then he might have felt differently. But Stu never did.

One Monday in September Bobby came by, still carrying the idiotic dog under one arm, wanting to tell Eric all about some Health and Safety course he'd been on. Summer was over and the foreign boy was back at school: a big improvement.

'Health and Safety?' Eric scoffed. 'What do you want to learn about that for?'

Bobby said that he had to because otherwise Jobseekers would have cut him off, but he'd found it interesting. 'They tell you a lot of facts.'

Eric was tying up some dahlias. The weather was turning and there was plenty of work to be done: deadheading, pruning, raking up the leaves that fell from the lime tree.

'When I was your age I was in the army,' he told Bobby. 'You want to try telling the army about health and safety. Snipers taking pot-shots at you. Land mines. Booby traps.' In fact, Eric had spent most of his time as a cook in the Royal Logistics Corp, but that was nobody's business but his own.

'OK, OK,' said Bobby, 'but just see if you know the answer to this one. What's the definition of an accident?'

Eric grinned. 'You know well enough when it happens to you!'

Wrong, said Bobby. An accident was an unplanned event that caused harm to a person or equipment. 'And what's the most common cause of accidents in the workplace?'

'Idiots.'

Wrong again, said Bobby. 'Slips, trips and falls. And the cause of most fatal accidents?'

Eric shrugged.

'Falls from a height. And do you know the definition of a height? A height is anything above ground. If I stand on a brick I am working at a height.'

'Get away!'

''S true,' said Bobby. 'And if you're down in a basement and you step up on a brick? What's that?'

Eric didn't bother to respond to this. What was the matter with everyone these days? Doing lessons and courses and tests and trying to make him feel bad? He felt bad enough already. He pinched the bridge of his nose to stave off a wave of dizziness. Maybe he'd caught a bug? When he'd bumped into Stu down on the high street the other day, Stu had made a big fuss about how skinny he'd gone. 'You want to get that checked out, Eric,' he kept saying. 'You're a bag of bones, man!'

Bobby was still droning on about this course: acceptable upper limits for noise in a work environment; the legal minimum temperature for indoor and outdoor working – on and on he went. Eric could feel a headache getting going on the right side of his head, a low hum, like a Flymo skimming across some faraway lawn. Stu had made him promise he'd go and see the doctor. It was true that he'd gone down a notch on his belt recently and there was the dizziness and sometimes bouts of nausea. But why should he go to the doctor and be found wanting yet again? Not heavy enough, not steady enough: always failing. No, he wouldn't do it.

Eric looked up. Bobby and the little dog were watching him expectantly, as if they were waiting for him to speak.

'What?'

'I said, do you know the legal maximum? The legal maximum temperature?'

Eric hesitated. He could see what was going on. Bobby was trying to make a fool of him. Even the dog looked as if it was primed to burst out laughing. He'd say something and then the pair of them would start cackling. Well, he wasn't going to give them the satisfaction.

'I'm not answering a ridiculous question like that.'

'The thing is, right? There IS no legal maximum temperature!' Bobby doubled over as if this was the funniest thing he'd ever heard. 'They can send you to work inside a volcano and you can't say nothing about it!'

Eric turned his back on the two of them. 'Ridiculous,' he muttered to himself. 'Doesn't make a bit of sense. Who's going to ask you to go and work in a volcano? What do you take me for?'

When he looked again, Bobby was heading up the hill, head tilted, one leg dragging, the little dog clasped under one arm.

An unplanned event: that's what I was, Eric thought.

At four o'clock, Mrs M came out of the house with his mug of tea, bursting to tell him her news. Thomas's mother had called to let her know that Thomas had passed the first round of tests. 'I can't tell you what an achievement that is, Eric. Thousands of children take these tests and only about a third are chosen to go on to the next stage. Oh, it really is wonderful news!'

Eric nodded, but his mind was elsewhere. All afternoon he'd been thinking about her again. He didn't know her name or age or anything, just that she'd left him in the Ladies at Waterloo. His key worker had told him the story when Eric was old enough to ask. A foundling, they said. Well, that depended on how you looked at it. From his perspective it was more a case of lost than found.

Only when Mrs M had gone back into the house again did Eric realize that she'd forgotten his biscuits. He tried to get back to raking the leaves but he was too upset. Was her head so full of the doings of this foreign boy that he, Eric, should go without? He wasn't expecting luxury. He wasn't asking for chocolate-coated or foil-wrapped. He only wanted what was due to him: a couple of digestives, a rich tea, a garibaldi perhaps. Did he not deserve at least that?

He went up to the front door and rattled at the metal grille. 'Mrs M!!' he yelled.

For a while there was silence in the house. He hammered and yelled some more and at last she came to the door. But she didn't unlock the grille.

'What's the matter, Eric?'

They stood there, looking at one another. It was so quiet that he could hear the scuttling of dry dead leaves on the path behind them.

'Is something wrong?'

Such stupid things she was saying. Of course something was wrong. He opened his mouth. He knew what he wanted to say: Let me in. I want to come inside. Open the door for me. But when he spoke, the words came out in the wrong order, nothing but jumble and blurt.

'Outside,' he said.

No, that was wrong.

'Upside.'

Wrong again.

'Inside out.'

He saw the puzzlement in her face. 'What's that Eric? Say again?'

And then behind him came the squeak of the garden gate and Mrs M was looking beyond him, one hand at her throat and a wobbly smile on her lips. It was the Polish boy coming up the path with a sturdy blonde woman who looked just like him.

'Mrs McClusky! We have brought some cakes!' The woman held up a white box tied with ribbon. 'To say thank you for all your good help!'

Eric was exultant. Now Mrs M would have to open the metal gate and he would get to go inside the house. At last, at last! Maybe they would invite him to sit at the table with them? Maybe even offer him some cake?

He bounded up to the top step, caught hold of the metal grille and swung around to look at the boy and his mother. It was a syrupy golden autumn day. Everything in the garden looked so beautiful. Sunlight glanced off the boy's high clever forehead and set fire to the yellow helmet of his mother's hair, lighting an answering blaze in Eric's skull. His eyes turned inwards. It was as if he passed through so many different times of his life, falling in and out of quite distinct sensory envelopes: the dreary magnolia of the children's home; the classrooms of his infant school with their scratchy navy carpets; the periwinkle taste of swimming in the municipal pool; the desperate sweaty muddy stink of basic training; the slippery pink tang of that girl he'd gone with in that alley in Belfast, the one who looked so like a boy and whose name was lost to him now; the perfect black stillness of the warehouse on his 2 a.m. rounds; the breathless, brackish taste of fear; all the hues and scents of Mrs M's garden on so many days and in so many different seasons. He put his hands to his head and before he knew it, he was having an unplanned event. He was toppling. He was falling from a height, just as Bobby had explained it. He tried to grab hold of something, but he had gone too far. He had passed the mid-point.

He was lying under clean sheets in a bright warm place. He couldn't open his eyes. It felt almost like being under water. He couldn't move, but he could hear the comings and goings of the people around him: footsteps, the squeak of a trolley, women's voices calling to one another in the distance. He had always liked the sound of women's voices.

There was a swish of a curtain being pulled on a rail and then Mrs M was right up close to his ear. 'Eric? Eric, can you hear me?' He could smell the powdery scent of her make-up. He wanted to answer but he was so tired. It didn't seem to matter. He hoped she could see that he was smiling. He was happy that she'd come. He forgave her everything. He was floating. He was still falling but he wasn't going anywhere. The curtains swished again. He heard Mrs M talking to another woman far, far away. Their conversation filtered through to him like sounds from the bottom of a well: '... sent off for tests ... fairly well advanced must have been suffering for quite some time ...' And then, 'Oh no, there's no question of discharging him. We'll be wanting to keep him here.'

Mrs M started talking about 'next of kings' and morphine, but Eric wasn't listening any more. He was lifted on a great ocean swell of happiness, his ears filled with the roaring sound of it. This was all he needed to know. He had passed some tests. He was advanced. And this invisible, faraway woman wanted to keep him. That was all he needed to know. He was on his way now. Yes, yes, indeed.

It wasn't her fault, thought Corazón. She'd gone along to the audition quite light-heartedly, just to keep Tessa company. She couldn't be blamed if she'd ended up getting the job. Now everyone was annoyed with her, including Tessa. But what could she do? The director had already sent her the draft script with her lines highlighted in yellow, and they were going to pay her *money*. It was quite miraculous and amazing, and most amazing of all was that Robert couldn't be pleased for her. All he said was, 'I can't believe that I've spent half a year writing a play for you, and you're planning to go and work for someone else.' (Work for he said, as if she was some hired thing – that hurt.)

She found him out on the balcony, staring at the view. Their flat was on the seventh floor of a high-rise; you could see for miles in the gaps between the other blocks. It had been mild lately but now the sky was turning a heavy purple in the distance and the air was suddenly damp and cool. She went and leaned herself against him.

'Don't be cross,' she murmured, 'I hate it when you're cross.'

He said nothing.

Corazón moved her cheek against his shirt. She closed her eyes and imagined how they would look to someone watching. There might be someone looking across right now from the walkway of the next block. She knew they made an attractive couple. They were about as different as two people could be, and yet on the outside, from a distance, they looked alike: small and dark and wiry; that pleased her.

'Let's go to bed,' she murmured.

For a while he was silent, perhaps considering the idea. On the ground below everything looked squat and drastically foreshortened. A youth swaggered across the pock-marked grass with a pit bull straining on a short leash. Some younger children were pulling the bark off what might one day have become a tree.

'It's Wednesday,' he said.

'So?'

'We can't just up and go to bed in the middle of a Wednesday afternoon.'

'No?'

She brought her body closer to his, resting her chin on his shoulder, slipping her arms around his waist, lifting the shirt away from his skin. Robert had a very straight back, thin but strong. He didn't move. She could feel him breathing. She ran the flat of one hand across his stomach, just touching, brushing across the hair at his navel. A plastic bag drifted slowly down from the eighth floor, splayed open in the wind like a jelly-fish. Corazón slid her hand down further, dipping her fingers in under his belt. He shook her off violently. He went back into the flat.

Down on the ground one of the children had another in an armlock. The pit bull lifted its leg against what was left of the sapling. Corazón spat over the edge of the balcony, and watched the droplet gather speed and weight, barrelling down onto the bald grass. In the distance the sky gathered itself more tightly.

In the evening Robert lay on the sofa talking to his friend Anna for hours, not bothering to lower his voice.

'Cora's been offered this supposedly fantastic job – a new theatre company – they're called TNT!' He left a pause for Anna to fill with laughter. Corazón could hear them both – laughing and laughing. 'I'm serious. Tech-ni-cally Not The-atre: TNT.' The laughter grew nearly breathless, then died away slowly.

'They've got a grant to do a reworking of *Shakespeare* with some smarty-pants young director, you know – video cameras strapped to the armpits and microphone implants in their teeth, that sort of thing.' He laughed again, waited while Anna said something, then more laughing.

Corazón sat in the bedroom trying not to listen. It was sad, she thought, the way Robert said 'young' as if it was a tribe he would never join again. She lifted her head and looked at her reflection in the mirror on the other wall. She practised making it go dead, then come alive again: dead, alive, dead, alive. She blurred her lashes together till her face became a biscuit-collared pool with two ink-slash eyes. She could still pass for early twenties. Just about.

She got out her small collection of press clippings and spread them on the bed. There were none for the first play; a handful for the second and the third:

A brave production, energetically performed by the young company, notably Corazón Macmillan as Linda. The play itself begins to unravel after the first act

Corazón Macmillan as Linda is a talent to watch

The combustible Ms Macmillan as Maria brings an oriental flavour to an otherwise very English evening

Corazón Macmillan's Maria is an entrancing combination of narcissism and tenderness

'No, no, that's all up the spout,' Robert was saying. 'I'll have to cancel … Well, she's accepted it already … Yes.'

Corazón could almost hear Anna saying: 'Poor Rob. Can't you just get someone else?'

Most of Robert's friends were too sophisticated to look down on her. There had been one in the early days who'd got drunk and asked Robert if she was a catalogue bride, but he was more of an acquaintance really and Robert stopped seeing him after that. The rest of them made special efforts to include her in conversations. They alluded lightly to the Pacific Rim countries, talked on and off about identity and Diaspora, but she knew that they found her a bit light, her skirts too short, her laughter too loud, her education too sketchy. They were disappointed that she had never been to the Philippines, that her father was a white man, that her mother was an accountant and not a reformed prostitute or peasant. Robert said she imagined these things, but she knew she could never be like them, nor different enough to interest them. And they never laughed at her jokes.

Corazón folded away her cuttings and went into the kitchen. There was washing-up from the day before waiting by the sink. She ran hot water and washing-up liquid into the bowl and plunged her hands in, shivering at the loveliness of the heat. She thought about the two plays. Robert's was a sparse four-hander about a mixed-race woman passing for white in London in the 1950s. He'd written it especially for her – a gift of a part. But it would all take place in some tiny back room of a pub in front of a handful of friends. It would be like singing in heavy traffic, running the wrong way up an escalator. It would get her nowhere.

The other play was described as 'a response to The Tempest: an experimental multi-media event combining actors, dancers and video clips'. They had a grant to develop it in London, then tour it round the country, doing schools workshops in the day, theatre performances at night. Robert said it was bound to be terrible. But she would meet new people, learn things, build up contacts; she would be paid. It was easy to see what she should do. Anyone could see it, except for Robert.

She heard the phone in the sitting room click back into its cradle. After a while she sensed rather than heard Robert in the kitchen behind her, padding about in his socks. Corazón passed the sponge across a plate, scooped it round the innards of a mug, skimmed along the rim of a glass. She felt him watching her.

'Rob,' she said softly, without looking round, 'can't you just try and see it my way for a minute? I'm not doing this to spite you or get back at you or anything.'

'I'm not stopping you, am I?'

Corazón said nothing. She watched the light rocking on the surface of the bowl of water.

'Am I trying to stop you? Go ahead. Feel free. Just don't expect me to join in the celebrations, that's all.'

She glanced up at his reflection coming and going in the mirror that hung above the sink. She felt a cramp of guilt. He didn't enjoy being on the margins any more. He longed for a homecoming, attention, applause. He thought she could help him get that. Shouldn't she be touched at his faith in her? It would be so easy, she thought, to give in and have him take her in his arms right now. All he wanted was that she give up a smallish part in an experimental production. Was that so very hard for her to do?

Robert stopped at her shoulder.

'What?' she said, lifting her head. Their eyes met in the mirror. She imagined the acute angle of their look, like a broken bone.

'I said I washed that already. That glass you've just washed. It was already clean.'

She opened her hand so that the glass splashed back down into the water. 'What is it?' she whispered. 'What's eating you up so?'

'Loyalty, Cora. Either you feel it or you don't.'

Five years ago she might have picked up the glass and thrown it at the wall. Now she gripped the sponge under the water where he couldn't see.

'Don't worry,' he said. 'I'm going out.'

'I won't be bullied, Robert,' Corazón shouted after him. 'I won't!' She'd given him six years, she thought. He had no right to ask her for any more.

When it got dark, Corazón heated a can of soup and spooned it straight from the pan. After that she went into the sitting room and rang her friend Emily, lying on the floor and talking for nearly an hour. She weighed up the two play scripts. Robert's was considerably fatter. Maybe it was just the kind of paper he used. She felt wistful.

'He's changed,' said Corazón. 'He used to like the way I rushed into things, even if half of them went wrong. He used to say I inspired people, you know, the people we worked with.'

'You do,' said Emily, 'you do.'

'These days he's always finding fault – the way I breathe when I'm sleeping, the way I do the washing-up. He says I'm noisy and untidy. He says I always burn at least one thing when I cook.'

'Poor honey,' said Emily.

Corazón felt tears of self-pity start in her eyes. Emily was so much nicer than Robert. Why couldn't she fall in love with Emily instead?

'Sometimes I think it's his friends,' she said to Emily. 'That Anna. She and Michael have always had it in for me. They just want him all to themselves – especially her. They hate me.'

'Oh come on now!'

'She does. I know she does. I can't help it if I'm not ugly, can I? Or short. She might have been able to tolerate me if I was a dwarf – like her.'

'Co-ra!' Emily was laughing.

'Well it's true, isn't it?'

Corazón balanced both scripts on the soles of her feet. She lay there looking at them, poised above her head.

'Would you say I was childish?' she said in a small voice.

Emily stopped laughing. There was a silence.

'Robert says it was understandable when I was twenty but I ought to have matured more by now.'

Emily clicked her tongue. 'You two have been working together too long, that's all. You've been through worse.'

'I'm not sure,' said Corazón. 'Maybe this is different.'

Another silence. Then Emily said quietly, 'It wouldn't be the end of the world, Cora. There are things you could do on your own that you will never do as long as you're with Robert.'

What? Corazón wondered. She felt a wave of desolation. She remembered the beginning, before they were lovers, when she'd seen him and known at once that he was the one she wanted. In those days she hadn't yet learned to censor herself and words still had free passage from her brain to her mouth. She'd pursued him quite shamelessly, barging uninvited into parties and picnics and weekends away until at last, lying beside that slow-moving yellow stream at Anna's parents' house, she'd got him to kiss her. She could still see it now: sunlight skewering the water, poplar leaves tapping and clattering lightly overhead, everyone else asleep and Robert rolling across the grass towards her. And when he kissed her, everything fell into place. He'd become her place of abode, her domicile, her single state. How could Emily say that it wouldn't be the end of the world?

Corazón drew in her legs and let the scripts slide to the floor. 'I'd better get off the line,' she said because she thought she was about to cry.

'You hang in there,' said Emily. 'And call me whenever you want.'

'OK,' said Corazón.

At ten o'clock Robert rang to say that he was over at a friend of Tim's, and there were a couple of people there who might go on to Anna's or they might just stay where they were, but either way, he was too drunk and tired to make it home. He didn't sound particularly drunk but nor did he sound as cold as before, just ordinary. Corazón could hear people laughing in the background.

'That's fine,' she said brightly. 'Thanks for letting me know.'

The laughing was probably nothing to do with her, but still it wasn't a nice sound.

'Love you,' she said.

He hesitated for a moment. In the background came the sharp crack of a beer can. Then he said: 'Bye.'

What else could he say, she thought afterwards, in the

middle of a crowd?

She woke just after dawn with the bedside lamp still burning and a book crushed under her head. She couldn't go back to sleep. She got up and went into the kitchen to make herself a cup of coffee. There was no milk in the fridge, nor any bread.

She realized suddenly that, because Robert had fallen into the habit of doing the shopping, she had no idea of what they had and didn't have in the way of food. The fridge was empty except for a carton of yoghurt and some floppy carrots. She looked hopefully in the store cupboard. There were a couple of bags of dried beans, a tin of fish, two tins of tomatoes, and, right at the back, a dusty packet of table napkins. Corazón reached in and retrieved it. It looked as if it had been there for years, probably left behind by the previous tenants.

These beautiful and durable two ply cocktail napkins, it said on the back of the packet, *can be used when serving hors d'oeuvres, as finger wipes or as drinks coasters. Choose from our range of eye-catching primary colours or subtle pastel shades depending on the occasion or the mood you wish to create.* She stared at these words for a long time: *the mood you wish to create.* For some reason she thought of her mother.

The sky was quite bright by now. She shook herself and tossed the packet back into the cupboard behind the jars and tins. She would go out and get some bread and milk from the shop in the 24-hour taxi place, she thought. A piece of toast and a coffee would make the world more manageable. She slipped into her shoes and her jacket and went to open the front door. It wouldn't budge. She fiddled with the catch, shoved it in, then twisted, pulled and lifted, rattled, pushed and tugged it over and over. Nothing worked.

'Christ!' she shouted, kicking the doorjamb, turning on the door itself until her foot was numb. She slid down onto the floor and sat listening to the silence settle. The understanding broke slowly. Without thinking, Robert must have locked her in when he went out the night before. She fished her mobile out of her pocket and called his number; almost at once his ringtone sounded in the room behind her: he'd left his phone behind. She slid down onto her haunches beside the door, head on her knees.

She must have dozed off like that because the post seemed to come out of nowhere, rattling through the letterbox in a rush of sharp, wet air.

'Wait!' she yelled, scrambling up and calling through the flap. 'Excuse me! Wait a minute please!'

The postman had already begun to walk away. She heard his footsteps slow momentarily. She yelled again, 'Excuse me! Could you come back a minute!'

The steps faltered.

'I'm locked in,' she called. 'Could you help me please. I can't get out of the flat.'

There was a silence now.

'I'm trapped!' she yelled.

The silence dragged on, full of doubt.

'Help!' she called. 'Let me out!'

That seemed to decide the matter. The footsteps resumed at once, rapping off along the walkway at a great pace, growing steadily fainter and fainter until they were quite gone.

It was easier to attract the milkman's attention because he had to bend down and collect the empties before he left the fresh pints, and she had a nodding acquaintance with him. He'd been doing the round for years, not like the postmen and women who came and went. He was obliged, at least, to answer when she called.

They were both squinting sideways through the narrow slit of the letterbox, each bent at the waist. She could see his eyes and nose and the shoulder of his white coat; his peaked cap. He considered her with grave caution. Somewhere in some respectable house he had a respectable wife and you could be sure she'd never found herself in this situation.

'What is the problem exactly?' said the milkman with a carefulness bordering on distaste.

'My boyfriend went out last night and locked me in by mistake. It's the Chubb lock, you see. There's no Chubb keyhole on the inside. If I could just pass the keys out to you ...'

Perhaps, in a situation like this, she should have said 'husband', but she had trained herself not to use the word because Robert despised such petit-bourgeois pretensions. 'Marry?' he always said. 'What for? Why sign a contract drawn up by the state?' It wasn't as if they had a child or anything.

'Last night?' said the milkman.

'Yes.'

'You've been locked in all night?'

'Well, I must have been, though I didn't know it until a minute ago.'

'I never like to get involved in trouble between a man and a woman,' said the milkman through thin lips.

'You don't understand. There's no trouble. It was just a mistake.' Corazón could hear herself getting panicky. 'He's usually the last one out. He's used to locking the door. It's his habit, that's all.'

'You never know the right or wrong of it when comes to couples,' said the milkman, straightening up a little. She could no longer see his cap, just his mouth and nose. 'You get mixed up and try to help one and next thing they both turn on you.'

'It's nothing like that!'

'But I can't agree with locking women up,' the milkman muttered. 'Can't agree with that. Not in this country.'

'Come on, please! I just want to get to the shops and get some bread for breakfast. I'm hungry.' She tried to laugh but she knew there was a pathetic whining note creeping into her voice. For no reason at all the phrase from the napkin packet came into her head: *the mood you wish to create.*

'Go on,' said the milkman, sighing irritably, 'give me the keys. Just don't tell him it was me. I'm retiring in six months. I don't want any trouble.'

When he'd gone, Corazón leaned in the doorway, listening to the ever-fainter clink of milk bottles disappearing down the walkway. She looked at the packet of cocktail napkins lying at her feet and she was nearly overwhelmed with grief. What a disappointment she must be to her parents. A girl who never gave cocktail parties or served hors d'oeuvres or thought about creating moods through colour. What was it that she had in place of all the things her parents had wanted for her once? Robert?

She put one foot, then the other, across the threshold, but somehow with the way it had happened she no longer felt like going out any more. She would have the air of someone on probation, someone who had to be very careful not to have their privileges rescinded. Why couldn't she have been more imperious in her dealings with the milkman? More dignified?

She ran out into the middle of the walkway and yelled at the milkman's white departing back, 'I'm not a mail-order bride, if that's what you were thinking!'

He didn't turn around.

'Men!' she hissed furiously through her teeth. 'Bastards!'

She shifted back and forth from one foot to the other, crossing and recrossing the threshold. There was an elastic fury bouncing inside her. She ducked down and grabbed one of the fresh pints by the door, turning to go inside. Then she changed her mind. She came out of the flat running. She flew right up against the balcony rail before she let the bottle go. There was a crash from below; but already she was swinging back for the second bottle. She flung this one high and far, and the milk came out of its shell, making a beautiful ragged arc against the sky before it sagged and fell.

There was a brief moment of elation. She felt as if she

73

had struck a blow for the meek and the pretty, a blow for all those who couldn't think of the right words at the right time, who lost arguments, who were struggling to escape from bonds of their own making, for those who had nothing and no one but themselves to blame for it. Then she went to the edge and looked down at what she'd done. In the back of her head she heard her mother's quick hurrying voice: 'You have a bad temper, Corazón Macmillan. Men don't like that. If you are going to get on – even in this country – you'll have to learn to control yourself.'

When Robert came back he found her lying with her eyes half closed on the sofa with the two play scripts balanced on her stomach.

He threw his keys on the table with an easy swing, then went into the kitchen and put the kettle on. Corazón watched him through the service hatch. She could see that his mood had changed. He had a boyish tilt to his movements. His face was open and unrumpled.

'Some idiot's been smashing milk bottles out there,' he said. 'Could have killed someone.'

Corazón turned her head away. 'Nice time?' she said.

'It was OK,' he said. She heard him getting out the cups, measuring the coffee into them. The spoon rang out clearly against the china. 'Met some interesting people. Another bloody war correspondent and a couple of actors – well, an actor and an *actress* to be precise.'

He came back into view through the glass hatch, smiling a little. Something had fallen into place for him, she thought, something had been fixed or settled last night. She wondered when he would decide to tell her about it. She saw him open the fridge and look in. Then he frowned. She felt an inexplicable wave of loneliness.

'What's happened to the milk? Did he forget to deliver?'

'You just passed it. Down on the path.'

He stared at her in disbelief. 'Both pints?'

She shrugged. He shook his head, laughing to himself. When he'd made the coffee he came back into the sitting room and perched at the end of the sofa by her feet, still smiling.

'What is it?' He shook his head. 'Not because I didn't come home last night?' He peered down at her with something like tenderness, rubbing at the ends of her toes.

She had been ridiculously jealous in the early days, but that seemed a long way off now, someone else's emotion, only Robert hadn't noticed that she'd changed. She shook her head.

'What then? You're not premenstrual are you?' He ducked like a man avoiding shrapnel. 'No?' He carried on laughing for a bit before he quietened down. 'Sorry,' he said. 'You OK?'

'I'm fine,' she said. She felt him watching her. He put out a hand and caressed her knee.

'You look pretty today,' he said, 'almost pink-cheeked.'

He ran his hand higher on her thigh and let it rest. Corazón didn't move. It was amazing, she thought, that he could not see how jagged and full of temper she was. She wondered what the actress looked like, whether he'd found her attractive.

They sat in silence for a while. He shifted his hand gently on her leg. She didn't move.

'Want to go to bed?'

Corazón considered the question. She wanted to be smoothed and stroked and calmed but not particularly by him. She wanted to stop being angry but not like this. Robert put his coffee cup down on the floor and let himself fall across her legs, his arm curled around her knees, his head resting in her lap. She felt a disconnected shudder of desire. Her eyes closed. She put out her hand to touch his hair. Some people liked to be tied up, she thought.

He wouldn't understand, she thought. It wouldn't mean anything to him: being locked in. If she'd done the same to him, he'd have been briefly annoyed, the way he was

75

when she forgot to put the top back on the jam, but nothing more. He'd have switched on his computer and got on with his work. Work. Suddenly Corazón's eyes flew open. She knew now what had changed his mood, why he'd said: 'Well an actor and an *actress* to be precise'. He'd found someone to replace her in the play. She dragged her knees out from under him, struggling to her feet.

'Hey! What's the matter?'

Now there would be no more talk of loyalty or principle or conscience. He would encourage her to take the job with TNT. He would be pleased that she was bringing in some money. It was all so neatly solved, so incredibly tidy.

'Get a grip, Robert. It's Thursday,' she hissed, swinging her hair behind her like a rope. 'We can't just go to bed in the middle of a Thursday.'

For a moment he stared. Then he rolled into the space she'd left on the sofa, covering his head and pretending shame. 'Cora, Cora. My merciless Cora!' He kept laughing, waiting for her to join him. She half wanted to, but she was angry. It was all very well for him to be sweet now – now that he didn't need her any more.

She looked at him, lying there, his handsome face turned towards her, amused and unguarded. Right now he wanted her to forget, but when it suited him he would come back to this job as an example of her fickleness and vanity, he'd hold it up as a test of integrity failed. He could talk you mad, Robert. He could prove that up was down. And how could she complain? It was what she'd loved about him once.

Corazón walked over to the window and looked out at the concrete view. The clouds raced like dogs across the big sky. There was a Londis bag blowing among the pigeons; a smaller scrap of paper whirling away – someone's bus ticket perhaps. What did they have to show for all these years, she thought? Just a folder full of scrappy little cuttings and a packet of someone else's table napkins in a rented kitchen. No house, no car, no child. Not a tie in the world. They were absolutely free and unfettered, both of them. This was how he'd arranged it.

He lay on the sofa still, watching her lazily.

'The original escape artist, that's what you are, Robert,' she said softly under her breath, 'the original bloody escape artist.'

'Eh?' he sat up and looked at her, still laughing. 'What did you say?'

But she was silent, thinking of all the things that lay out there beyond the edges of this view: other people, other places, other ways of living. Right now I could just about die of sadness, she thought. I could sink. On the other hand ...

She thought of the improvisation they'd done in the afternoon of the audition, the new director yelling, 'Reach right in and tap that rage, Cora. Use the emotion! Use the whole of the stage. Travel!' And suddenly, far off in the distance, she saw a bigger, more untidy and exciting life where no one would mind if she left the top off the jam and couldn't cook. I could be good, she thought. I could be so bloody brilliantly good it's just ridiculous. I know it.

'Eh? What?' Robert said again. 'What's so funny? Why are you laughing?' He held out one arm. 'Come over here, you crazy bird.'

But she stayed where she was at the window, smiling out at the speeding, tumbling sky. And in the room behind her a puzzled silence grew, active as a storm of bees.

LIVE SHOW, DRINK INCLUDED

'How much?'

'Ten pounds,' said the woman behind the hatch. She looked surprised, sitting up there on her high stool. She crossed her legs and the leather skirt cut into the flesh of her upper thigh, all blue and white and mottled – like council wallpaper. Neal looked away.

'Ten pounds?' Gayle looked at Neal. 'What do you think?'

'If you want,' Neal murmured. He still couldn't quite believe they were going to go through with this.

They'd been walking around ever since the coach dropped them at Victoria at 10 a.m. – Oxford Street, Regent Street, Piccadilly Circus, Buckingham Palace, Leicester Square, Chinatown – Neal couldn't remember half of the places they'd been. And then suddenly they found themselves in this little side street full of flashing neon signs and Gayle was saying: 'Why don't we go in here and see what it's like? Just for a laugh!' and: 'It'll be an experience'. Neal wasn't at all sure it was the kind of experience he wanted to have, but today was his birthday present to Gayle and anything she wanted she must have.

'Ten pounds,' Gayle was saying to the woman in the ticket booth. 'Does that include a drink?'

'Ticket includes a drink of your choice from the bar and a live show.' The woman seemed uncomfortable, tugging at her orange tank top, avoiding their eyes.

'You're sure, now? There's not going to be anything else we have to pay for?' Gayle was bent double trying to speak through the tiny gap in the glass where only hands and cash were meant to pass. Her lips were nearly through to the other side. 'Could you just write that on the ticket for me, please? "Drink included." Here, I've got a pen.'

They climbed a narrow flight of stairs till they came to

a small landing where an enormous shaven-headed man appeared and took their tickets. He indicated that they should step past him through the open doorway, which was covered only by a bead curtain. It was like slipping into dark water. Neal felt his stomach lurch.

The room beyond was ordinary: black-painted walls, chairs and tables on one side, and a small mirror-tiled bar in one corner. The smell was somewhere between a public phone box and a betting shop, with undertones of something else. There was piped music, a cheerful Pointer Sisters song. The bald man went over to the bar and, without asking, poured them two watery-looking halves of lager.

'That'll be five pounds each,' he said, gazing fixedly at a point somewhere above their heads.

'No, that's not right,' said Gayle.

'Five pounds,' the barman repeated, still not meeting their eye. 'Look at the drinks menu if you don't believe me.' There was a snake tattoo curling all the way over the muscles of his upper arm to his collarbone; the red lights rattled on the dents in his skull.

'No, honestly. I asked the woman on the door about this. And it says here on our tickets. See? "One free drink".' The barman moved towards Gayle with a threatening expression. Gayle didn't flinch. He looked right at her. He stared. He took in every single thing about her: her scrawny shape, her dead-white skin and dyed black hair, her nose piercing, the spider tattoo on her upper arm. Then he straightened up and shoved the two beers roughly towards them. 'This way then,' he said.

He showed them to a table in the furthest, darkest corner of the room. Gayle tried to argue for somewhere nearer the door but the barman just said, 'I don't think so,' and Gayle caved in immediately. The business with the drinks seemed to have taken it out of her a bit. The two of them sat down and the barman headed back to the bar.

'What if we want to leave?' Gayle called after him.

'Leave?'

'In the middle of the show? What if I don't like it? How do we get to the door?'

A faint shadow of surprise drifted across the barman's face. 'Same as when you came in.'

'Yes but what about …?' The sharp note was back in Gayle's voice. 'This is going to be a live show, isn't it?'

He nodded.

'And where …?'

The barman pointed to a dirty strip of carpet that lay in the centre of the room.

'Oh,' said Gayle. 'So close?'

'Just step over them if you want to go,' said the barman. 'They won't mind.' He retired behind the bar and started cleaning half-pint glasses with a tea towel.

Neal reached over and squeezed Gayle's knee. 'OK?' he whispered. Gayle was still staring at the patch of carpet in the middle of the floor.

'I can't imagine what this is going to be like.' A frown appeared between her eyes. 'I'm worried.'

Neal sipped his drink. 'Why?'

If Gayle really wanted something, Neal tended to switch off and let her get on with it. Most of the time it didn't matter to him what came next, whereas almost everything mattered very much to Gayle. Why make a fuss? Some people misunderstood this easy-going side of his nature. When he was in Year Four his teacher had more or less told his Mum he'd never amount to much. 'I won't say lazy, exactly,' this teacher said, 'but the word "competition" certainly isn't in his vocabulary.' Neal couldn't see a problem with that. Why should everyone be competitive? What was the point?

'I'm worried I won't like it now,' Gayle said. 'Do you think they'll have clothes on?'

'I don't know,' said Neal.

'What if they have really ugly bodies?'

Another man came in and sat at a table by the door.

The barman brought him his drink and the woman from the ticket booth appeared and ordered a drink too. The song came to an end and then, with a click, began all over again. Jump! buzzed the Pointer Sisters. Jump for my love.

Gayle bit her nails and glanced at her watch a few times, though it was too dark to read the face. 'I should have got that luminous one in the market the other day,' she muttered.

There were so many things Gayle wanted – not just wanted but genuinely seemed to need: luminous watches, china frogs, plastic flowers, kaleidoscopes, brooches, painted tea trays, fridge magnets, key rings. Each new thing would be perfect for a time, but sooner or later whatever she saw in it would be used up and she'd be off looking for something new.

Perhaps that was why she wanted to come here, Neal thought. He looked around him at the black walls and the bare floorboards, then at Gayle: ramrod straight, eyes darting about the place, her mind whirring. What was she looking for, he wondered? Was this just a random impulse, or had she been planning it all along? An unnameable fear gripped him like a cramp.

Gayle was the one who'd made all the moves at the beginning of their relationship. Neal didn't understand at first. He'd always been on the heavy side and a bit shy of girls. He thought Gayle was just naturally friendly. In the end she got tired of waiting for him to catch on and just turned up on his doorstep with two little plastic suitcases. He'd been in bed with bronchitis at the time. That was nothing to Gayle. 'I can't wait any longer,' she said. He remembered the feel of her in his bed, her breasts so soft and her knees so hard, all pressing against him as she talked. 'Don't you see it, Neal? Don't you see how we belong? Fat and thin, yin and yang, quick and slow – together we make one thing? Do you see what I'm saying, Neal?' (and him nearly unconscious with the combination of fever, desire and surprise). 'Me with no parents and you with

82

both. And look at the numbers – NEAL and GAYLE – N is the seventh letter in the alphabet and G is the fourteenth: two sevens are fourteen. And our birthdays, Neal ...' She was always looking for patterns, Gayle. She believed that everything had its place in the world: a perfect fit. But things could change. The loveliness of the plastic trinkets nearly always wore out in the end. Perhaps she was the same about people? Perhaps after all this quiet time she wanted someone darker and more exciting – a demon lover? Neal did a quick rummage through the cupboards of his soul, looking for undercurrents and licentious thoughts, handcuffs, whips – he found nothing worth mentioning.

The barman crossed the room to the other table. He leaned in and said something to the man in the coat, handing him a piece of paper.

'I wonder if they'll change the music when the show starts?' Gayle murmured. 'Do you think they'll have it with music or without? Oh, I'm really nervous now.'

'We can go if you want,' Neal said hopefully.

Suddenly the man at the other side of the room was on his feet and yelling really loudly. 'Are you CRAZY?!' he roared. He overturned his glass, nearly overturning the table. 'You must be JOKING!'

Gayle jolted. Neal reached for her hand in the dark.

Over by the door, the newcomer made a lunge for the exit. Swift as a ballerina, the tattooed barman moved to block him and the ticket-booth woman followed. All three were shouting at the tops of their voices. Then, as suddenly as it had begun, the argument was over. The woman went back downstairs. The barman and the customer drew close and something changed hands. The man left. Behind the bar, the music clicked off, then began again on automatic replay: 'Jump!'

'What's the matter?! What's going on?!' Gayle called to the barman in a squeaky voice. Her fear ran like a current into the palm of Neal's hand.

'Let's leave,' he whispered. 'Let's just get up and go

before there's any more trouble.'

But the barman was already on his way over to them, striding across the room. From the ground floor came the sound of a door or a fist slamming. Neal shuddered. What if they should both just disappear today? Nobody from the village would think of looking for them in a place like this. Nobody even knew they'd come to London. Oh who could save them now? The barman loomed above them, huge as a mountain and twice as terrible. Gayle's hand trembled inside Neal's.

'Look,' said the barman. 'Let me explain something to you.'

They came stumbling and blinking into the brightness of the street, rubbing their eyes.

'I thought you were going to insist on seeing the show,' Neal said, 'I mean, we'd paid ten quid and everything.'

Gayle shook her head. 'What would be the point? I'd already worked out who it would have been.'

'Who?'

'Who was doing everything else in there?'

Neal thought about the barman with his marble eyes and his solid, wardrobe-like body, and the woman in the ticket booth with her variegated flesh – Sandra, the barman had called her – Sandra and the barman: working.

'I don't want to sound like a body fascist, but to be honest ...'

'I know,' said Neal quickly.

They started walking now, in the direction of Leicester Square. Neal felt a bit dizzy, as if his head had just been released from a vice. 'This place isn't meant for people like you,' was what the barman had said at the very end of their talk. 'You don't have good jobs or reputations to keep up. You don't care who knows you're here. Do you see what I mean?' Gayle said she appreciated his frankness.

Neal slowed a little to let someone pass. He found himself looking into the faces of the other people around him: men in smart jackets, young women with long hair, tourists with slow open faces, all sorts. For a moment he thought he had stumbled into an extraordinarily attractive clump of people, but then he understood that it was more an accident of perception – for some reason he was only seeing the beautiful bits of people right now – just the lustre of this one's skin or the shape of that one's head; this step or that smile. And most beautiful of all was Gayle.

Neal watched her crossing the road ahead of him: the swing of her skinny arms, the hopeful set of her shoulders, the way she held her head up, looking people in the eye: always full of anticipation. It was amazing the way she'd turned out, he thought, considering all the hurts and disappointments she'd had.

She turned back to him with that busy, serious expression that meant she had a new idea: 'You know, Neal, there's always the waxworks. We've got that half-price voucher for Madame Tussaud's. Remember?' she yelled across the roar of the traffic.

Neal stepped out to meet her. A car swerved, blaring angrily, forcing him back onto the pavement. Gayle came halfway back to meet him, stopping on the traffic island in the middle of the road. 'If we hurry up and get the tube we should be able to squeeze in a visit before it's time to get the coach,' she was yelling.

He hitched at his belt. 'Hang on,' he said.

Before he even knew it he was out in the traffic again. This time he was fearless. He put on some speed and lumbered towards a black cab which was gone by the time he reached it so that he just had enough time to lurch out of the path of an open-topped sports car. He felt its slipstream caress the seat of his pants. Then he threw all his weight forwards to avoid an enormous touring bike bearing down on him at speed. Gayle caught his hand and, through a combination of her pulling and him falling, he made it safely onto the traffic island. He straightened up and as he did he had the sense of something lifting away from him, a dark cloud moving away into the distance. I'm safe, he thought. She's safe. We're both safe. There is no demon lover.

'Jesus, Neal. Be careful, will you. So, what do you want to do?'

Neal reached out and hooked the hair behind one of her gigantic ears. He felt idiotically happy. 'About what?'

'Not about anything, stupid. What do you want to do now?'

I can't really think of anything else I want, he thought: just to have her beside me in bed at night, standing next to me in the bathroom in the mornings, eating breakfast and setting off for work, going to the launderette and the supermarket on the weekends. What more could I ask for? If you cut me open with a little knife there'd be a print of her right there in the middle of me. He brushed the stubby ends of his fingers across her cheek.

'You choose,' he said. 'I'm easy.'

A Minor Disorder (South Africa, 1956)

They had been driving all day and by now they were in an
endless, undulating sort of chicken-scratching landscape.
There was so much space with so little in it that Stefan
became afraid.

'We must get more water and a can of petrol in the next
town,' he said to Jonas, 'in case the car breaks down.'

Jonas did not respond. Since their last argument it
seemed he was pretending to be travelling alone. Suddenly
he pulled the car over to the side of the road, switched off
the engine, got out and began to walk away.

'Where are you going?' Stefan called.

'For a walk.'

Stefan watched him stride away across the dry, flat
land. They had never really got along, not even at school.

Stefan, too, got out and walked some way in the other
direction. He squatted down on a low rock and looked
about. What at first appeared to be a pathetic, poverty-
stricken emptiness grew more complex when you studied
it for a while. A stream of fat red ants passed close to his
shoe. He became aware of the high, machine-like singing
of a thousand insects. Bees. Crickets. Something glinted
briefly in the scrub about a metre away from him and he
wondered whether it might be a snake. He wasn't at all
afraid. How far we have come in these past eight weeks,
he said to himself, much further than just the distance
between Sweden and Africa.

Sitting here on the rock in the middle of the veldt, he
began to feel glad for the first time. He felt a starburst of
happiness in his chest. Ten days into a new continent, two
weeks short of twenty-one – what a life there was to be
lived in such a brilliant light.

Something made him turn and glance back at the car.
He saw Jonas climbing in at the driver's side. A moment
later the engine coughed into life. In his mind, like a

snapshot, Stefan saw that copy of *L'Étranger* sticking out of Jonas's bag, and the hunting knife he carried in his coat. Then he stopped thinking and began to run. He'd been a champion cross-country runner at school. He reached the car and tumbled in just as Jonas began to accelerate.

'You swine, Larsson!' he panted, forcing a laugh.

Jonas said nothing, just swung the car back into the middle of the road. The sky above them burned.

By nightfall they were in the Karroo proper: a dry, secretive place. They stopped in one of the larger towns where there was a hotel with a bar full of white farmers, red-faced and roaring. There was a little hatch at one side where the barman stuck his head out to sell bottles to the black labourers in the street. The hotel owner's daughter showed them to their room, unlocking the door and snapping on the light so that the moths and mosquitoes shot about crazily in the air. There was a huge speckled tile floor with four beds ranged against the walls like a school dormitory, each one covered in a pastel-shaded bedspread with tassels (sick-pink, blue and green). It was like a hospital or a prison, Stefan thought, with a wave of despair. It was hideous.

Jonas went off to have a shower. Stefan chose one of the beds and sat down with his suitcase, close to tears. He longed with an almost physical pain for his mother's high-ceilinged Stockholm flat with its beautiful parquet floors and Kelim mats, the elegant chairs, the black and gold lacquer cabinet that Uncle Sven had brought back from China, the silk curtains that had once hung in their house in Malaya.

Stefan opened his suitcase, lifting out the stacks of neatly folded shirts and trousers till he came to his books: a French novel, a couple of English sheep-farming texts, an account of Linnaeus's botanical expedition to the Cape in the 1700s – new books for the future, old ones to remind him of home. The one he wanted was right at the bottom of the case: a battered medical encyclopaedia that his mother had given him as a parting gift, *The Universal Home Doctor (Illustrated)*. She herself had been given this book by an Englishwoman in Malaya before he was even born, and she had consulted it faithfully about all their childhood ailments till he and Harald were old enough to go away to school. Now she had handed it on to him, her only surviving child. Stefan touched the worn cover with the tips of his fingers.

'You will not find a book like this today,' his mother had said. 'People will tell you that there is such a thing as progress, *mon cher*, but I'm not sure I agree: dances are shorter, men are less handsome, encyclopaedias have fewer entries. Let this book be your guide, my dear; it will keep you safe.'

It was as close to an expression of tenderness as she would ever get.

Dinner was served from half past six in the dining room behind the bar. A few minutes after they'd sat down a small yellow-skinned woman in a pale pink cotton uniform and matching head-cloth appeared from the kitchens. She carried a tray with two platefuls of food which she set in front of them without a word: thick slices of meat in gravy, fat grey peas, carrots, roast potatoes and a sweet sticky root that Stefan couldn't identify.

'Thank you,' Jonas said in his careful English, smiling.

The woman looked startled and scuttled back to the kitchens.

'They've probably never seen foreigners in this town,' Jonas said.

Stefan thought of the light, clean tastes of his mother's table – potatoes with dill, grilled white fish, ham baked in pale cream sauce. He forced a cheerful smile and loaded his fork. 'I'm starving!'

'Again? Have you got worms?'

Stefan pretended not to hear. He'd decided it was the

best strategy.

The kitchen doors opened again and the little woman appeared with a bottle of chutney, which she put on the very furthest edge of their table. Then she was gone again. Jonas followed her wistfully with his eyes.

'Perhaps she speaks only Afrikaans,' he murmured.

'Perhaps.'

In fact, if he was honest, Stefan was finding the whole business of servants more discomfiting than he'd anticipated. Almost everywhere you went in his aunt and uncle's house in Cape Town you bumped into a retainer of some sort: two maids in the house, a gardener outside. No doubt on his uncle's farm it would be even worse.

When the woman brought them their dessert – thick peach halves swimming in a single great clot of cream – Jonas addressed her haltingly in Afrikaans, '*Wat is jou naam*? Your name? *Jou naam*?'

The woman backed away from their table with an expression of fascinated horror, like someone confronted by a freak-show creature in the wrong context.

'*My naam* is Jonas, *en dit is* Stefan. *En jy*?' Jonas pointed. '*Jy*? You?'

'Regina, *baas*,' she whispered.

Jonas flinched. '*Baas*?!'

Stefan closed his eyes. They'd been through all this already in Cape Town with his aunt and uncle's maid.

'I am not your *baas*, Regina …' Jonas was saying. 'My name is Jonas Larsson. Just plain Jonas Larsson.'

'*Ja baas*.' The woman glanced back at the kitchen doors.

'For God's sakes, Jonas. You're embarrassing the poor woman.' Stefan muttered.

Jonas threw him a slaughtering look.

That night a vague ache in his stomach kept Stefan awake. Hour after hour he lay there listening to the distant roar of the white farmers, and then, when the bar closed, to the sound of Jonas snoring. For some reason, he was haunted by the memory of his uncle's gardener in Cape Town: a tall and melancholy man with clothes that flapped against his bony frame. He saw the gardener reaching out to skim leaves from the glasslike expanse of the swimming pool, his frame bent in two like a croquet hoop by the nature of his work, his skin both leathery and soft, burnished by all weathers, his hat pulled down over his eyes. When he smiled, his mouth was cavernous, surprising. What kind of a house did he live in? How far did he travel on that rusty old bike of his? Did he have children?

After a while Stefan rose and went to the toilet at the end of the corridor, but he produced nothing. Back in the room he stood at the window to catch the light of the streetlamp and read the entry for Parasites (worms) in *The Universal Home Doctor (Illustrated)*. His skin turned cool: round and flat worms, thread and jointed, burrowing, drilling, microscopic – the number and variety of intestinal parasites was beyond belief.

In the morning he went down to the desk to pay for their room while Jonas packed the car. Stefan leaned against the desk, feeling strained and exhausted. The owner's daughter took his money almost without counting it. She was around eighteen years old and very strong. He'd heard her in full throat that very morning, tearing into one of the women in the kitchen. But in his company she was reined in and tremulous, as if he sapped her strength.

She leaned forward on the desk, her forearms squeezing against her breasts, and asked if they'd be coming back. Stefan said he thought not. The girl sighed and stared as if she was pressing him into an image that she'd keep for another time. Her mouth hung open a little. Stefan could see little flecks of her breakfast caught in her teeth, something red and not quite cooked.

From the road outside Stefan heard the first rough cough and stutter of the car's engine.

'Excuse me,' he said. 'Goodbye.'

How would he know if he had worms? Stefan leaned his head against the metal rim of the window on the passenger's side, feeling it jouncing his brain as they drove. Would he actually feel the creatures quickening and wriggling in his gut, sucking and whirling, draining his life's blood?

Beside him, in the driver's seat, Jonas whistled softly between his teeth. Suddenly he began to recite in his stilted singsong English: 'We the people of South Africa declare for all our country and the world to know that South Africa belongs to all who live in it, black and white, and that no government can justly claim authority unless it is based on the will of all people … that our country will never be prosperous or free until all people live in brotherhood, enjoying equal rights …' he broke off and looked at Stefan. 'Do you know where that comes from?'

'No.'

'It's the preface to what they call the Freedom Charter.'

Stefan adopted a strained, enquiring expression.

'I see.'

Stefan thought of the worms, making highways in the heart of him, and he felt faint. His head was like ice. 'Do you think we could stop in the next town and see if there's a pharmacy?'

'What is it *now*?'

'Nothing serious. I'd just like advice about something.'

'From these ignorant sods?' Jonas snorted. 'On your own head be it, my friend.'

The grey-green landscape unrolled itself on either side of the road. There was a hawk or some other bird of prey circling on the horizon. Stefan thought of the hotel owner's daughter in the place they had just left and he sighed.

'Perhaps I'll wait until we get to a bigger town.'

At midday they stopped the car and got out to eat the sandwiches the hotel had provided. It was another burning day. They had a bottle of water and two packs of sandwiches wrapped in wax-paper: meat with sweating daubs of butter breaking through the bread.

Jonas took a square and examined it before he took the first bite.

'Even their bread is white.'

'No need to go on about it all the time.'

Jonas stopped perfectly still. Then he leaned in and stared at Stefan, his jaw working as he ate. It seemed to Stefan that Africa was doing Jonas no good.

'You find all this quite normal, do you?'

Stefan shrugged his shoulders. 'We knew what we were coming to. It's not a secret. You talk as if you'd only just found out about the situation here.'

'To *know* and to *understand* are two very different things. Didn't you hear that woman last night? Didn't you hear what she called me? "Master". Doesn't that frighten you?'

Stefan sighed. In Sweden now, he thought, his breath would leave a white smudge on the air; here it was dispersed into the sweetness without a trace.

'Jonas,' he said, 'we are new to this place. We may not really understand all the things we see and hear. There are customs, rituals, there's a history to all of this. It may be feudal but so was Sweden once. Things will change, but it requires some patience. Until then, there is at least security of some kind here, order.'

Jonas laughed. 'Order? Hah! Where have we heard that word before?'

Stefan flushed irritably. 'I don't know what you mean.'

Jonas was on his feet. '*Ordnung! Ordnung!*' he shouted, '*Die neue Ordnung meine Damen und Herren!*' punching out a salute, laughing wildly.

Stefan's cheeks burned. 'I'm no Nazi. My family worked with the Danish Resistance right through the war …'

'Of course they did. Nazis probably wouldn't be well-bred enough for your family.'

'My Uncle Sven was tortured for ferrying Jews across

to Sweden, you know ...'

'Oh, why don't you just shut up. I'm sick of hearing about your family.'

Jonas walked a little way away, then squatted down to finish the last of his sandwich. Stefan sat folding and refolding the waxy sandwich paper, squashing it between his thumb and forefinger till his nails went white.

'Why have you come here, Jonas?' he said loudly. 'To atone for the sins of the world? To bring revolution? To bring salvation? Are there not enough poor people for you in Sweden?'

Jonas shook his head and looked away, a sarcastic smile on his lips.

Stefan was boiling now. 'D'you know what you are, Jonas? Wait! Wait a moment, I'll read it out to you!' Stefan ran back to the car and dragged the medical encyclopaedia from his suitcase. He went back to where Jonas squatted in the middle of nowhere.

'*Megalomania*,' Stefan read. He was trembling with this unaccustomed rage, 'insane conceit ... the exaggerated belief in one's own power or ability ... The person who suffers from megalomania in a mild form is the typical "reformer", who sets out to put the world to rights, according to his own point of view ... Before the real nature of his trouble is realized, he may have recruited an army to rescue an oppressed nation, or ...' Here he had to stop because Jonas was laughing too loudly to hear him any more.

'Insane conceit, eh?' Jonas wiped his eyes. 'And what do you propose instead? Eh?'

Stefan shrugged. 'Abiding by the law, working hard, being kind and courteous wherever you can to everyone regardless of their colour or nationality or class. Living your life as well as you can in your own small way.'

'How charming,' Jonas said abruptly. 'And how many people must die, quietly and politely out of sight, before you abandon this genteel and gentlemanly niceness?'

'It's not niceness, it's …' He was about to say 'decency', but Jonas cut him short.

'Nice, nice, nice!'

'Stop it!' Stefan found himself shouting, although the emptiness around them seemed to swallow the sound at once. 'It's what I believe!'

'Ah-ha! Of course you do!' Jonas yelled. 'How charmingly, uselessly NICE of you!'

Stefan lashed out blindly. 'Shut UP!' His fist connected with Jonas's shoulder and, to his surprise, Jonas toppled back without resistance. There was a crack as his head hit a small stone. Then silence.

'I'm sorry,' Stefan whispered.

Jonas didn't move, just lay there with his eyes closed.

'I don't know why I did that. It must be the heat. I must be out of my mind. Please forgive me, Jonas. I didn't mean to hurt you.'

Jonas didn't stir.

The sun was blasting down on them, but Stefan felt frozen inside. Could this be death? Did it come as easily as this, from one careless gesture? He thought of everything that must surely follow now: grim officials, handcuffs and rough words. His mind buckled. His breath sobbed in his throat. Oh God! In my heart I didn't imagine anything like this! I'm not a bad person. I'm not a criminal. This was not what I meant at all! But how to explain that in a strange, wild place where no one knew him. Mamma! Merete, save me! Tell them who I am. Don't let them take me away! But Mamma and Merete were far away from him now.

Stefan forced himself to be calm. He felt for a pulse in Jonas's wrist and found it after all, blood knocking against his fingertips. This was not death, though it was bad enough – Jonas stayed so very still. Hours seemed to pass. Stefan kept his fingers stubbornly on his companion's pulse until, without warning, Jonas's hand snapped round and caught Stefan's wrist in a ferocious grip. He jerked and Stefan found himself half-lying across Jonas's chest.

'Idiot!' Jonas hissed, his eyes glittering with an unnatural light. A piece of spittle struck Stefan on the cheek. Jonas wouldn't let him draw away. One hand held his wrist while the other had him by his shirt collar, almost strangling him. His eyes looked crazy. Sunstroke, thought Stefan, or some kind of swamp fever? From the corner of his eye he glimpsed *The Universal Home Doctor* lying open in the sand, just out of reach.

'When are you going to open your gummy little eyes and see how it is here? Do you know how many people die every year of TB and dysentery in this orderly paradise?'

'I … I don't know,' Stefan stammered.

Jonas stared at him; then he smiled and said in a closer, more confiding tone, 'I could very easily kill you now, you know. I could make it look like an accident. I could say you slipped and hit your head. Think of it. They would never suspect me. What would be my motive?'

'Jonas,' Stefan croaked hoarsely. His brain was all disordered; thoughts came and went quite inappropriately. He saw in great detail the windowsill in Aunt Merete's room, with all those unpleasantly hairy-leafed violets in their Chinese pots. He thought of the girl who'd put her tongue into his mouth when he kissed her at one of his farewell parties in Stockholm – he couldn't even remember her name. He saw the picture of his father in British Army uniform, the last one taken before he died. He thought of the gardener at his uncle's house in Cape Town who took nine spoons of sugar in his tea.

'Jonas,' he wheezed, 'why would you want to kill me? What would it achieve? How could you go and teach in a mission school with blood on your hands?'

Jonas stared, then abruptly shrugged Stefan off him and got to his feet. 'You're right.' He began dusting down his clothes. 'Your death would serve no useful purpose – there would only be ten more self-deluding little men like you to flood in and take your place. That's the trouble with the world.'

Stefan lay back against the hot earth, weak with relief. How good of Jonas to spare him, how beautiful that he was not going to end here, crushed in the sand like a snake or a rat. I must see all of this clearly, he said to himself. I must remember this day. This is the beginning of my new life.

'You know, Stefan,' Jonas said.

'What?' Stefan whispered, still lying on the sand. Jonas turned to look over at the car that stood like a lump of burning tin on the road. Stefan followed his gaze. He felt an irrational weakness almost like love flooding through his limbs.

'You know you have a choice. You can think for yourself. You have a brain. You can get involved, take action. But your trouble ...' Jonas sighed. 'Your trouble ... your trouble ... Do you *know* ... what ... your *trouble* ... is, *Stefan*?'

There were birds singing in the distance, and a high buzz of cicadas and crickets in the clumps of dead yellow grass. The sun shone on their white-blond heads and the pages of *The Universal Home Doctor* rose and fell uncertainly in the breeze (*Megalomania, Melancholia, Memory*). It had never occurred to Stefan that Jonas might have any medical knowledge, but why not? Perhaps you needed to know the basics in order to teach in a mission school. (*Mercurial Poisoning, Mesmerism.*) Stefan felt suddenly alert and hopeful, almost excited to hear the diagnosis.

'What?' he murmured. (*Monomania, Mountain Sickness, Myopia.*) 'What's my trouble?'

And the wild flowers trembled against the dryness of the veldt.

Laura didn't look up but she could feel Natasha travelling towards her across the open-plan office like an electrical storm.

'I've had it with this guy,' Natasha said, slamming a file on Laura's desk. 'You'll have to take over. Take him to lunch. Bat your eyelashes or whatever it is you do. I've got to focus on the Bookfair.' She walked off without waiting for a reply.

'Tell her no, Laura,' Anna hissed. 'The book is way behind schedule and it's all her fault. Don't let her dump it on you.'

Laura ran a finger over the pale brown cover. *Dark Knights and Fair Ladies: Tales from the Court of Love.* She didn't like to turn down a challenge. Besides, Natasha wasn't someone you said no to.

The author was a medieval historian. Laura had noticed him when he was still working with Natasha, a spiky, ungainly, middle-aged man with a kind face and a loud laugh. He wasn't laughing when they met for lunch, though, and Laura knew why. It was all in the file, a catalogue of badly managed disputes.

Laura had chosen a quiet little restaurant. She ordered a soothing egg dish, boiled greens and spring water. The author glared and demanded steak and a beer: food to sustain a rage.

The company Laura worked for published glossy illustrated books on art and architecture, certain kinds of history, popular science, posh food. Laura, Natasha and Anna were employed to make the text fit into the spaces between pictures and to make sure it sounded clever without depressing the reader by being difficult. To do this they had to make a lot of changes. The authors were generally specialists or obsessives – people who knew little about the marketplace.

To Kevin, the managing editor, authors were a necessary inconvenience. Clearly, he believed he'd have done a much better job of all the books if only he'd had the time to become an art historian or a wildlife expert or a baker of artisanal bread. As it was, the authors handed you the raw material and you turned it into a decent product and then (first stop) you had to sell it back to the authors as being their own work. This was where Laura excelled. She reasoned and explained. She consulted endlessly. She strained every fibre to get her authors to embrace, enjoy, even, the salami-slicing of their work. Sometimes it meant that in the bargaining they managed to slip some of their more abstruse passages back in. Kevin didn't always find out. Natasha's style was different. She simply ripped out what she needed and threw away the rest, too bad if her authors didn't like it. Natasha was at her best with people who had a weakness of some kind, people who needed money, or publicity, or a publishing credit. With this type of author Natasha produced really excellent commercial work.

You had to remember, Kevin always said, that readers were busy people, or if they weren't busy they had a short attention span. To compete against games and social media and online shopping, books had to let go of their excessively linear quality. A book, said Kevin, should no longer be seen as something that sat on a shelf reproaching you for not having finished it. A book should be like a saucer of sweets, each chapter brightly wrapped and inviting in its own right. You could eat your sweets in any order. You could go back and forth, dipping in and out of the bowl depending on your mood. And whatever applied to the thing as a whole should apply also to its parts. The eye, said Kevin, should be able to move effortlessly around every page, taking in little parcels of information ranged at so many different levels – in the sidebar, the text boxes, the pithy captions to illustrations – like treasures in a smart

100

shop. Their books aimed to be big but not bulky, serious but not heavy, beautiful but not intimidatingly so.

Sitting in the restaurant Laura tried to explain some of this to the author without alarming him. 'And you've got such great material!'

He laughed mirthlessly. 'But? There's always a but, isn't there?'

Laura took a deep breath. 'It's over-length. We have to be much more selective: foreground the narratives, drop a lot of the background stuff. And ...' She hesitated. 'We mustn't forget that, however encoded, it's a book about sex, isn't it?'

The author looked shocked. He took another mouthful of steak. 'You're as bad as the other one,' he muttered. He set down his knife and fork, still chewing. He rubbed his knuckles against the side of his head. 'We are not talking about a period in which individual desires were of much consequence. These "romances" were a strictly circumscribed social ritual. It was a culture that licensed amorous friendship, not sex. Of course there were probably liaisons but that is not the point.'

'Of course,' said Laura. 'We can certainly make that clear.'

'"Too excessive a habit of pleasure prevents the birth of true love". That's article 29 of the Code of Love. Now, that may be a foreign concept for someone of your generation ...'

'Let us call it passion, then,' said Laura evenly. 'People will be looking for the stories about passion. Sublimated or not.'

The author looked as if he wanted to kill her outright.

'Look, I know you've written lots of academic books, but this is something different. We need to find ways of making your expertise accessible to our readers. They're the only reason we can offer the kind of money you will be getting.'

She met his gaze and held it, unblinking. I will be your

friend, her eyes said. I will carry you through this if you let me. And he looked back just as steadily. The moment went on and on, far beyond politeness. She saw that he was susceptible to women, that he was impulsive and oddly naive, a poor judge of character, that he had been badly let down in the past. She saw that he was torn between liking and hating her and in that particular moment it wasn't in her power to influence the outcome.

He wiped one hand over his eyes. Then he grinned and made a faintly insulting joke about Natasha that Laura couldn't help laughing at, and she knew she'd begun her work. She might even bring him in in time for next year's Christmas list.

In January Laura and the author met for the second time. They sat in one of the meeting rooms, which were really just cubicles at one end of the open-plan office, boxy places smelling of unnatural fabrics and glue.

'So?' The author shifted in his chair, wary as a boxer.

'It's still too long.'

'Dammit, woman,' he yelled. 'I've cut everything I could possibly cut. What more do you want? Organs? Limbs?'

'I do have some suggestions.'

'I'll bet you do.' He leaned back, arms crossed, glowering. After a while the temper left him and he just looked at her. 'How old are you, Laura?'

'Twenty-eight.'

'Christ,' he murmured. He wiped his hands over his face. 'OK. Come on, let's have it, then. Do your worst.'

When they had gone through all her notes they put away their papers and went out to one of the local coffee bars and they talked about other things. He told her about his latest battle with management at the northern university where he taught, and about his family. 'Here, look!' he fished in his wallet for pictures: a boy of eight, a girl of ten and a slim woman with long reddish hair. Laura studied the image of the woman, who until now had been no more than a voice at the end of the phone. ('I'll just get him for you'; 'He'll be back in an hour'; 'Can I take a message?') She looked much younger than the author and possibly quite pretty; her face was turned away from the camera and the kids were climbing all over her so it was hard to tell. In the background, Laura caught a glimpse of a substantial red-brick Victorian house and beds of wispy flowers. The house, she knew, was the reason he was doing this book. It needed serious work.

'Nice,' she said.

He smiled and nodded. 'My wife is a film scholar. Much more up to date than me. You'd like her. You'd like each other.'

Laura was startled. How could he even *imagine* that they'd ever meet?

She caught Anna watching her sometimes, tight-lipped with disapproval. Anna was happiest when Laura was working with someone who drove her crazy. Then they could be allies, rolling their eyes and groaning when the calls came through. Anna would pull faces and try and make Laura laugh while she was on the line. There was none of that with this book.

When Laura rang to tell him that he was going to have to get rid of five of the images he'd earmarked for chapter four, the author broke into verse: '"Tepid and dark shall be the cold pure snow, / The ocean dry, its fish on mountains dwell, / Ere Love or Laura practise kinder ways."'

'What ...?'

'Petrarch.' He was laughing at the other end of the line, far away in the north. 'One of the sonnets. Never mind. Hack away, my dear, hack away. I am utterly without defences.'

She hung up, still smiling.

Anna was watching her from the other side of the desk. 'This is going to end in tears, Laura.'

Laura looked around. Several people were out at meetings. Natasha was off sick. No one was listening. 'Are you suggesting that I'm being unprofessional?'

Anna went red. 'I just think you're getting too involved.'

Laura pretended not to understand, though she knew well enough what Anna meant. There had been a day she should have gone to lunch with Anna and she had met with the author instead. There had been an evening when she and Anna should have gone to see a film and she had stayed late to talk to him on Skype. There were altogether more phone calls than could be justified, and far too much hilarity. Once or twice, as they sat discussing a particularly tricky section in one of the meeting rooms, people had come to complain that their shouts of laughter were disrupting concentration in the main room. When she was with him it felt as if the world was brighter, lighter, bigger. Where was the harm in that?

She called him about a couple of small matters to do with the final chapter. She knew his home number by heart now. She dialled, then leaned forward in her chair feeling her heart race along the line with each ring, flying north across the dark, damp countryside that separated them. She had travelled that way by train, once, long before she'd known him, and at the time had paid scant attention to the journey, but now when she made these calls she tried to reclaim little scraps of remembered scenery: billowing trees and brownish fields, motorways, the mangled ruins of abandoned factories – things he might see on the way down to London, or on the way back (home, she always thought, would take him longer – he'd be moving uphill on the map, against the current).

His wife answered: the auburn-haired film theorist; the mother of his children; chatelaine of the red-brick house.

'Hi! Hi there! It's Laura!'

'How's it going, Laura?' The other woman's tone was friendly but distracted. Laura got the idea there were other people about. She imagined a lunch party, people leaning in from another room raising eyebrows, mouthing: *Who is it? What do they want?* Then she heard a Hoover start up in an adjoining room and at once the imaginary lunch party dissolved and was replaced by a new image: a cleaner. His wife was a woman with a cleaner.

Laura could hear herself babbling: 'Everything's fine. The book is coming along really well but I need to check …'

'You know what, Laura, he's out with the kids right now – half term. It's all a bit hectic.' And then more distantly, over her shoulder into the room. 'No … not the … if you can just … hang on. Sorry, Laura. Shall I get him to ring you when he gets back?'

Out. With the kids. Laura felt the disappointment like a punch. 'Yes, please. If he has a moment. I can probably sort it out with an email, but I just thought … sometimes it's quicker to pick up the phone …'

'An email is probably the best idea. I'll tell him you rang.'

Laura replaced the receiver and sat for a moment staring at the phone. Dismissed. Distressed. Mistress. Missed stress. Mess. She feared the things that might be read in her face if anyone were to glance her way so she got up and hurried out to the kitchenette and made herself another coffee.

February came and went as the author struggled with permissions and got one of his post-grad students working on an index. Laura dispatched a book on urban wildlife to the typesetters, corrected proofs of a book on dry gardening and took delivery of a manuscript about jam and jelly-making ('One day my quince will come,' said Anna).

In March, the office was rocked by scandal. Natasha disappeared overnight, without warning. One day she was there and the next she was not. No one had a chance to say goodbye because she didn't even come back to clear her desk. They arrived for work one morning to find Natasha's possessions piled in a box in the middle of her desk and a friend came to collect it for her later. Kevin had all the locks changed on the same day, as if a thief had been.

People were stunned. Natasha had not been popular in the office but she'd been important. Everyone had had an opinion about her. She'd attracted hostility and temper like a lightning conductor. Without her there was suddenly a scary vacuum.

One by one, Kevin began to invite the remaining staff to drop into his office for a chat. When it was Laura's turn, she found him in the middle of a phone call. He nodded and waved her to a seat. Kevin was disconcerting because he was always moving and there seemed to be a hundred streams of thought jogging along in parallel in his head. He might suddenly stop in the middle of a sentence to scribble a note to himself on a pad of paper, or punch a button on his phone and fire a question at someone in another office. You had to keep your eyes on him to make sure that what he said was really meant for you.

'You've been with us a while now, haven't you, Laura?' he said when he'd finished his call. 'You're not showy but don't think you haven't been noticed. You did a great rescue job on the Love book. You really turned that around.'

Laura bit back an impulse to laugh. 'Thanks.'

'You could do very well here, Laura. But – a word of advice. Do you know the story of Bluebeard?'

Laura chewed her lip. 'Bluebeard?' She wondered whether Kevin might be having a bit of a breakdown. He and Natasha had been very close.

Kevin walked over to the window and glanced out over the shallow sea of flat roofs that constituted his view. 'New bride. Great big castle. Bluebeard has to go away on business. Gives the wife his bunch of keys. Great big bunch of keys to every damned door in the castle. It's like he's flattering her with his trust, letting her believe that they're a team. And then he says: just one small thing, could she please not use one of the keys on the bunch.'

Laura nodded. 'To the room where he keeps the bodies of all the women he's murdered.'

'Eh?' Kevin had the phone in his hand before it had even managed a full ring. 'Talk to me.' He listened intently for a moment then he said, 'No way. They can do better than that. Go back and squeeze 'em some more. Let me know what they say.' He hung up and looked blankly at Laura. 'Where was I?'

'Bluebeard,' Laura prompted. (If he has murdered Natasha I'd really rather not know about it. Please, God, let him keep it to himself.)

'Yee-es, Bluebeard. I'll tell you why that story is on my mind.' Kevin walked towards the window again.

Outside, two seagulls touched down on the nearest roof, squealing, and Laura thought of summer coming. She imagined the author at the seaside playing with his kids, making sandcastles while his red-headed wife looked on, probably wearing a broad-brimmed hat and a long-sleeved muslin shirt to protect her pale skin. Or perhaps he would go to the beach with the kids and his wife would go to the library do some research? Laura had looked her up. She had written lots of essays and a book on women in film noir. She taught part-time. The day before, Laura had rung the house about a file the author had sent. His wife picked up and when Laura explained about the attachment not opening the woman laughed and said, 'He's such a techno-klutz, isn't he? I'll get the kids to help him sort that out.' Laura thought she sounded nice, like the kind of person you would want as your friend. And that made her feel terrible.

Kevin was explaining that in business there was no room for sentiment. He had learned this the hard way. You had to be like Bluebeard's wife: looking behind every door, in every desk and file, taking nothing at face value. 'Understand me? There is no room here for anyone who wants to use my company as a "springboard" or a goddamned "launch-pad". I'm not paying people to come in and steal from me. I have a lot of friends in the business. If someone crosses me, I'll make damn sure no decent publishing house will ever touch them again. Do we understand each other?'

Laura nodded, but really she was still thinking about the day before, when she'd gone to a bookshop in her lunch-break and somewhere out of sight a woman had said, 'I'll just get him for you.' And the voice was so much like the voice of the author's wife: so helpful, trusting, friendly, unsuspecting, that it nearly brought Laura to her knees.

'Excellent,' said Kevin.

By the end of the week everyone knew that Natasha had been trying to lure away some of her authors and set up her own company. Kevin had got wind of the plan and had paid someone to hack into Natasha's phone and email accounts to get him the proof he needed. He had loved Natasha. She, of all the editorial staff, had always been closest to his way of thinking. She had always been the one he went to when he was unsure about something. Now he was merciless. He sabotaged her deal with the distributors. He won back the authors. He made sure the story got around in the trade and showed her in the tackiest light. It would take her years to start anything again.

The incident left its mark on office life. For a while everyone was jumpy, though most were guilty of no more than the occasional filching of post-its and pens. Anna began to talk about changing jobs. Laura knew that they would both leave eventually. It was not the kind of place you wanted to settle down in unless you were like Natasha. Or Kevin. It was a question of timing.

'Though I suppose I'd be complaining about something else in another job,' Anna said. 'We're never happy, are we?'

Laura couldn't help herself. 'That's what my historian says. He says if things ever get really easy you can be pretty sure you're dead.'

Anna looked away. 'Stop it, Laura.'

'What?'

'You know what I mean. Stop bringing him into every bloody conversation.'

Laura blinked and pretended to be hunting for something on her desk. The silence grew long and uncomfortable.

Anna sprang up and began to maltreat a vase of predatory-looking flowers on her desk, leftovers from a conference she'd helped organize the day before.

'I saw a job that would be perfect for you. One of the university presses. I'll email you the link.'

'Academic publishing pays too badly,' Laura said.

For a while there was just the rustling of the ugly flowers.

'You're not going to have an affair are you Laura?' Anna said in a low, angry voice. 'That would be too stupid.'

Laura screwed up her eyes in an effort to control her face. 'Of course not. What a cliché. Anyway, he loves his wife.'

Anna looked as though she might burst into tears. 'God's sakes! You haven't discussed it with him have you?'

Laura shook her head. 'No.'

Anna leaned in, her silver earrings swinging like bells against her jaw. 'Laura, I have been watching you. I can see what's happening. For some unfathomable reason the man has hypnotized you. You've forgotten where you parked your brain. I can't bear to stand by and watch you walk off the edge of a cliff.'

Laura shook her head. 'It's fine. It's nearly over, Anna. The book is pretty much done. Kevin vetoed the idea of a launch. Soon you won't have to hear another word about him.'

'Oh,' said Anna, falling back in her chair. 'Well … Good.'

The author stopped by to tell her about a mistake he'd found after he sent his proofs back. 'I had to come down to London anyway,' he said in an unconvincing tone.

The meeting room was occupied. Laura pulled up a chair for him beside her own desk. She was horribly aware of Anna sitting just a few feet away, pretending to read over notes.

'So you'll post me a copy whenever it arrives?'

'Of course. Several copies. Don't worry.'

'What are you working on now?' He seemed distracted, like someone struggling to keep himself whole under pressure.

She told him: *City Wildlife* was in the shops, *Dry Gardening* had gone off to the printers, *Jams and Jellies* was in proof. She was about to start working on a book about sailboats through the ages.

He laughed. 'Let's hope you get good weather for it.' He tapped his foot. He looked around the office. 'You know, if ever there's another war you should volunteer to interrogate enemy agents. You'd have them thanking you as they went to the firing squad. They might even offer to shoot themselves to save you the trouble and expense.'

'I made no changes you didn't agree to.'

'Precisely. You even had me making marketing suggestions by the end.'

'You want people to read it, don't you?'

'I want people to *buy* it. I'm not so sure I really want them to *read* it. Not anyone I know anyway.'

Laura blinked. It wouldn't occur to him that this might be hurtful to her.

'I was just thinking about one of the stories Natasha made me cut,' he was saying, 'the one about the twelfth-century Provençal poet. Do you remember that one? No? OK. Goes like this: there was this poet whose lady refused to speak to him, cast him out, because of some trivial offence. After two long years she sent a message to say that if the poet pulled out one of his fingernails and had it brought to her by fifty lovelorn knights, she might just be able to forgive him …'

'I think I can guess the rest,' Laura interrupted. 'As he put the pliers to his tender flesh she stepped out and prevented it because all she wanted was a proof of his love.'

'No, not at all,' said the author. 'It's not a story about faith. She did actually want him to rip his fingernail off and the poet knew it. So the deed was done and fifty broken-hearted knights trooped off and presented the bloody token to the lady, and so the poet was reinstated in her favour and their friendship endured for many long years. Great story, eh? Stendhal tells it in his book *Love*.' He was laughing. 'That's women for you, eh? They'd eat you alive if they could.'

'Rubbish,' Laura said. 'That's Stendhal's antediluvian view of women and maybe yours – but that's all.'

The author looked mortified. He leaned towards her. 'Was that a sexist remark? My wife keeps trying to re-educate me. She says I'll get myself fired one day.'

Laura didn't dare look across at Anna.

'It's fine,' she muttered. 'It's fine. Shall I walk you to the tube?'

She wanted to get the whole thing over with now. She couldn't bear it any longer. Perhaps he was trying to make it easier for her? Probably not. He wasn't very self-aware. It was part of his charm.

In the street, they passed through a flurry of pigeons and suddenly everything looked like a detail from an illuminated manuscript: a barrow of fruit glowing with grapes and persimmons; a man eating a plum the colour of dried blood; streaks of sun coming through the clouds like gold. I will have no more reason to ring or meet him after today, Laura thought. We will not bump into each other. We will not hear news through common acquaintances. I will miss him. I will want to pick up the phone. I will dream about him and wake up crying. It will be unbearable.

And yet Anna is right. He is a dinosaur. He is sexist and insensitive. He is not available. He wouldn't be right for me. He's way too old. He's a technophobe. He's a Luddite. But he makes me laugh. He's so funny and unpredictable. He makes me feel alive. But Anna is right …

At the station they were playing classical music over the Tannoy. The author stopped just short of the metal ticket barriers. Laura put her hands in her pockets and looked away, blinking. It was the music.

'It's none of my business, Laura,' the author said, 'but I'd suggest you consider a change of jobs. It's a terrible waste of time what you're doing there. Another few years and you'll start taking it seriously, like Natasha.'

She was offended all over again. She remembered something Anna had said after the best part of a bottle of wine: 'What we do may be superficial, Laura, but that doesn't make it easy.' The author wouldn't understand that.

She stared at an advert for rail-cards which said: *Get away from it all by train.* There was still time to change that. She knew that if she spoke carelessly enough he would agree to meet again – just to talk, just to talk. No harm in talking.

But already he was leaning in to hug her. 'Goodbye, Laura.'

She felt as if she was in one of those films where the explosion is played in reverse so that the building is sucked back whole again, every brick, every tile, every shard of glass leaping into place. Perfectly. She spoke into the tweedy space of his chest. He pulled back. It wasn't clear whether he'd heard. She wasn't even sure whether she'd spoken aloud; maybe she'd just made a sound. He touched her hair. 'Take care of yourself,' he said, and then he turned, and with a rattle of the barriers he was gone – back to the north and his meaningful work and his surprisingly young wife.

On her return, Laura paused in the lobby outside the main

office, blinking, trying to get her face back to working order. The sailboat expert had arrived early for their meeting and was standing chatting to Anna with an unseemly degree of animation. Laura couldn't bear the idea of either of them yet. She retreated to the gloom of the stairwell where they couldn't see her.

Tomorrow, she thought, tomorrow she would start looking for another job. She didn't want to have to be here when his book came back from the printers, didn't want to have to parcel up his copies and write his name on the label. Someone else could do that.

She would look for a job that didn't cost so much, something where you didn't need to smile so hard or give so much of yourself to people who were only passing through. Editing legal texts, perhaps, or business books? Tomorrow. She would do it.

She took out her phone. The author would be on the underground by now, travelling towards the station and the train that would take him home, back to that red-brick Victorian house that had become the castle of her imagination, though all of its rooms were always locked.

She hit a preset to conceal her call, then dialled.

After five rings his wife answered. 'Hullo.'

Laura felt everything inside her fly north, through all those drab towns and green fields.

'Hullo?'

Laura stood listening to the sounds of the household opening out behind the other woman's voice like an origami universe: hammering in the distance, a radio playing, workmen's voices. They were spending the money from the book. Already. Something fell with a loud clatter and the author's wife called, 'Be careful, won't you!' and then into the phone: 'Hullo? Who is this? Hullo? Hullo?'

Laura closed her eyes and waited for the click.

A man in his middle thirties came stumbling onto the top deck of a London bus, talking to everyone he passed as if he knew them. People looked up with dazed glances but as soon as they understood he was a stranger they gathered themselves into their coats and tucked away their eyes.

He flung himself into a seat at the front. 'That's better,' he said. 'What a day!' Everyone manufactured expressions of concentrated blankness except for the red-headed girl sitting across the aisle. She turned and smiled. She had a lovely smile, not at all intimidating. She had heaps of pale red hair piled up any-old-how on her head, pale skin and lazy red lips. She looked as if she had just stepped straight out of a warm bath and into the arms of the rich brown fur coat she wore.

The stranger registered her smile. 'I'm really tired out,' he said. 'I've been all over the place today.'

'Have you?'

'I have.'

His jeans and jumper were neat and new, his face was clean-shaven, but the initial impression of coherence disappeared as soon as he started to speak. He slurred his words and waved his arms – there really wasn't room for that kind of thing on a bus in the middle of winter.

'I was right up in the centre of town today,' he said to the girl. 'I went to see this man who wasn't there. I left him a note, see, because he wasn't there. Then I went to see another man who wasn't there. And he was in. So I stayed with him for a bit. Then I came back down south again to see about some business. And now I'm going home. I'm right tired out.' He shook his head. 'How about you?'

'I'm going to see my boyfriend,' said the red-headed girl.

'Ah damn,' said the man getting to his feet and peering out of the window. 'I've missed it now, haven't I?'

'What?'

'Brixton. I wanted to get off at Brixton and get the tube.'

'No, no,' said the girl. 'We're not there yet. We've only gone a little way.'

'Ah.' He sat down again. 'I wanted to get off in Brixton and get the tube to the Oval because that brings me right to my door, see. Not much of a walk. I've got no energy for walking. I had the flu over Christmas and all through the New Year – all that time.'

The girl smiled and nodded sympathetically, then she turned her gaze back to the road and sank away inside her brown fur coat. At first glance it looked like a real fur. No doubt most bears would willingly have slipped off their skin for a girl like this, though she'd never have dreamed of asking. On closer inspection you could see that it was fake.

'So where you off to then?' the man asked, looking wildly around the bus.

'I'm going to meet my boyfriend,' the girl said again. 'I'm a bit late actually. I was supposed to be there at five …'

'A bit late!'

The whole bus was listening now, straining to catch every word of their exchange.

'Yes. I got a bit delayed because …'

'A *bit* late?! You're more than a bit late.' The man turned and peered out of the dark windows of the bus. 'Don't you know what time it is? It's gone eight already!'

'No,' said the girl pleasantly, 'it's only just coming up to five.'

Everyone on the bus checked their watches.

'I shouldn't think so,' said the man. He turned to his neighbour. ''Scuse me, 'scuse me, mate. D'you have the time please?'

'Five past five,' said the neat Asian man in the window seat.

116

'Oh,' said the stranger, crestfallen, and then: 'I've been sick, see.'

'Don't worry about it,' said the red-headed girl. 'It's easy to lose track of things when you're rushing about.'

'I had the flu all over Christmas. Just couldn't get rid of it.'

'That's a shame.'

'I went to the doctor in the end, got them to test me because I wasn't feeling any better. I said to them, I said, test for everything: Hepatitis B, Hepatitis C, Aids, TB – the lot! Find out what's the matter.'

The girl nodded again. 'Best to be sure.'

'But the thing is, I haven't got any of them.'

'That's good, isn't it?'

There was a little silence. 'I'm HIV negative.'

'Well, that's good, isn't it?'

'Yes.'

'*Really* good news. A nice New Year's present for you.'

'It *is* good, isn't?' The man sounded surprised. 'Nothing wrong with me at all.'

The rest of the people on the bus turned away from the man and the girl now. They pressed their faces to the windows, pretending to stare at the glittering winter streets as if they feared that whatever ailed this man might somehow leak out and contaminate them. Bad news, they were thinking. This character is bad news.

The bus stopped and he leapt to his feet again, peering out of the windows at the road. 'Ah Jesus! No! I'm definitely going the wrong way here. I'm going completely the wrong … I want to go to Brixton … and this … this …'

'We are going to Brixton,' called the red-headed girl. But the stranger had already begun to stumble back down the aisle towards the exit, knocking shins and shoulders and heads as he went.

'Sorry, sorry …' he muttered, treading on everyone's feet. The bus started off again and he was still only halfway down the aisle. 'Christ, no!' he called, arms flailing wildly.

117

'Wait! Stop the bus! This is all wrong. I've got to get off!'

Several of the other passengers began to object loudly. One of them stood up and grabbed his arm: 'Take it easy, mate. You're *disturbing* people!'

'But don't you understand?' cried the stranger. 'I don't know where the hell I am. This is all wrong. I've got to get off now ...'

The more frantically he tried to hurry the more he became entangled in the coats and bags and umbrellas of the people around him.

'Ring the bell,' said someone. 'Alert the driver.'

The bus gave a sudden lurch. For a brief moment the stranger seemed to spin with an almost unearthly lightness. Then he fell, disappearing in a welter of arms and legs like a wild bird in a box of string.

Rich (Italy, 1980)

They'd been travelling for a couple of days already. Ashley's landlady in Rome had lent them her car, a Fiat 126, nearly new and fun to drive. Ashley paid for the petrol and Harry drove, but Harry was increasingly irritated by other aspects of the deal. By now it was four o'clock and most women would have begun to fret about finding a place to sleep – what with the recent bombing in Bologna and the general state of tension everywhere. Not Ashley.

Harry turned off the main motorway, still following the signs for Florence, and the sun sank lower and lower in the sky. In the end he was forced to say it himself: 'Time to stop soon, don't you think?'

Ashley paused in the middle of lighting another cigarette. She peered at him through a screen of long dark hair and smoke. She opened her lips but no sound came out.

'I don't want us to take a wrong turning in the dark,' Harry said. 'The carabinieri are pretty jumpy at the moment, looking for Red Brigades and God knows what.'

'Whatever you think, Harry,' Ashley mumbled; then in a studiedly casual tone, 'Maybe when we stop I could make a quick collect call?'

Harry just looked at her.

'OK. Maybe not. I guess you're right.'

They passed a sign for Fiesole and that set him thinking about an Italian girl he'd met some months earlier at a house party in the mountains: Claudia. Her parents had a place in this area. She'd given him her number, said to call if ever he was passing. His spirits lifted. It was worth a try.

They pulled up at the next roadside bar and went in. There was the usual payphone on the wall at the back. Harry dug out a *gettone* and dialled Claudia's number while Ashley ordered coffees, nodding and waving her hands a great deal. The men at the bar stared at her as if she was something out of a freak show. Ashley didn't seem to notice. Harry began to feel angry – both with her and on her behalf. On a day-to-day level Ashley knew so little about taking care of herself. Sometimes she talked about going back to the States and starting college; next minute she'd turn around and say she was going to be a waitress. It was laughable.

The ringing tone stopped and an older woman's voice came on the line. *'Pronto?'*

Harry turned to face the wall, concentrating. 'Can I speak to Claudia please?' he said in Italian.

There was a silence.

'Who is this?'

'My name is Harry. I met her in the mountains last winter. At Federico's place. If you just tell her it's Gianni Pescara's English friend.'

Another silence. He thought for a moment that they had been cut off. Then he heard the receiver being laid down and footsteps shuffling away to another part of the house. When Claudia came on the line Harry switched to English, which was perhaps a mistake because she was cold at first. Harry wasn't rattled. He kept talking to give her time to recall him. He talked about the beauty of the area, the peculiar emptiness of the roads, and how it had occurred to him, when he and Ashley found themselves practically on her doorstep, that he should give her a call.

'You just assumed I would be here?' Claudia said.

'I'm sorry?'

'Most of the time these days I am in Bologna. I arrived here only last night.'

'I apologize,' said Harry. 'We're intruding on a family occasion. I didn't realize.'

'It's OK. My mother is in this moment in France.' Silence. 'You said you are travelling with a girlfriend?'

'That's right,' Harry said. Another silence. He glanced over at Ashley. She was deep in conversation with a rough-looking man drinking brandy at the end of the bar.

'Have you eaten dinner?' There was a note of exasperation in Claudia's voice.

'Are you sure about this now?' said Harry, reaching for a pen and a scrap of paper on which to scribble down her directions.

'What I like about this country,' he could hear Ashley saying in her terrible, halting Italian, 'is that it's full of history. In America, where I come from, nothing is really that old, although we think it is. A lot of it is made of plastic.'

Somehow, the flame of the man's cigarette lighter caught a strand of Ashley's hair and there was suddenly a strong burning smell and a general commotion around the bar, people yelling and flapping their hands. The rough man looked distraught.

'It's OK,' Ashley was saying. 'It's really not your fault. This is always happening to me. *Non e problema*. Truly.'

At the other end of the line Claudia said, '*Ciao* Gary,' and hung up before he had a chance to correct her.

'So, you are making a trip?' Claudia said politely, looking at Ashley.

They sat facing one another across a glass coffee table, sipping the cheap red wine that Harry had bought along the way. The room was extremely clean but unhomely, furnished with a jumble of lightweight summer-house-style furniture and expensive ornately carved pieces, as if it had been thrown together by someone who wasn't paying attention. Rich parents, Harry thought. He'd seen it before, people he'd met at university.

'My grandmother was Italian,' Ashley said earnestly. 'I finished high school last year and my parents thought it would be good for me to … um … get away for a bit. I've been in Rome for a semester. Harry thought I should do some more travelling before I leave.'

'But of course.' Claudia looked disapproving. She flung herself back into her corner of the sofa, drawing her olive-green cardigan close as if it was cold, which it wasn't. Her light-brown hair flew out around her shoulders. She was truly beautiful, Harry thought, in that tight Gucci princess style. He tried to recall what she did. Her mother, Gianni had told him, was an opera singer and her father was some kind of impresario. Did Claudia sing? Would she expect him to remember?

'What places did you see until now?'

Ashley looked expectantly at Harry. She wasn't much interested in the physical world. She used travelling the way people used prescription drugs: to numb the pain.

'Orvieto, Assisi. Tomorrow we'll go in to Florence proper, then maybe Pisa, who knows?' Harry shrugged. 'She doesn't have to be back in Rome for another week. I have some time off work. I'm still teaching at the language school,' he added, in case Claudia had forgotten. 'I decided to stay another year.'

Claudia's features softened. *L'Italia è bella, no?* More beautiful than England, eh? Or America!' She laughed loudly, then with a little hooded glance in Harry's direction she said to Ashley, 'For a foreigner he is quite *simpatico.*'

Harry could feel himself relaxing, becoming handsome again. It was going to be all right. Women always came round to him in the end.

'Did you see many road-blocks?' Claudia was asking Ashley.

'I don't think so. Why?'

'I came here from Bologna yesterday evening. There were a lot of road-blocks. Because of the bomb. They were searching nearly all cars going out of the city.'

'A bomb?' Ashley looked stunned. She spoke enough Italian by now to be able to catch the headlines, but somehow she never did. 'What bomb?'

Harry coughed. If they started going into the whole business of yesterday's bombing – no warning, all those deaths, the random horror of it all – then Ashley would want to call her parents to tell them she was OK and they would order her back to Rome and the trip would be ruined. Luckily, at that moment the kitchen door opened and a stocky woman in jeans and a sweatshirt appeared. She spoke to Claudia in Italian. She was off home. When they were hungry they just needed to cook the pasta and reheat the sauce. 'You can manage that, can't you?'

Claudia was reaching for the older woman's hand. 'Come and say hullo to my friends,' she wheedled in a little-girl voice. 'This is Giovanna, my other mother. She has looked after me since I was twelve.'

'I'll be at the house if you need anything,' the woman murmured, extracting her hand. 'Don't stay up all night, now.'

'Sleep well, *tesoro*,' said Claudia. My treasure.

After they had eaten, Claudia took them out onto the veranda, which looked out over a long clear slope of land given over to vines. To the right of that was a little orchard of apple, peach and plum. Claudia sat on the first of a series of steps leading down to the vineyard, Harry and Ashley sat beside her. Harry caught the scent of Claudia's shampoo and the slightly girlish perfume she wore. He closed his eyes, floating.

'This place used to be only for weekends,' Claudia was telling Ashley. 'But since my parents divorced my mother spends more and more time here. I love it. It's so peaceful.'

'It's beautiful,' Ashley agreed, 'but so isolated. Are you not afraid to be here on your own?'

'There are neighbours through the trees on down there. And Giovanna and Enzo have the little cottage by the gate. But I like the solitude. If you cannot first be with yourself, you cannot be with others. It's true, no?'

'I guess so,' said Ashley politely.

Harry yawned. He glanced over at the Fiat where their bags lay on the back seat. Ashley had wanted to ask straight out if they could stay, but Harry said no. Freeloading was like a seduction; if you moved in too fast, or sounded too desperate, people were put off. You had to make yourself not care what happened, give them a little bit of power over you so that they could feel they had a choice. His parents were the other kind. They'd worked hard for everything they had and never owed anyone but the bank or the HP company, and then only for as long as they had to, every payment made on time: six months for a new sofa, twenty-five years for the house, five years for every car (always second-hand), no favours or special terms. What a joyless path.

Claudia took out a chunk of Lebanese black and began to roll a joint with neat efficient fingers. 'You want to smoke?'

'Why not,' said Harry, laughter leaping in his throat.

The joint passed from hand to hand in a kind of ceremonial silence. Harry closed his eyes. This was what he loved: the risk of accepting gifts, the unknowable free-fall into the pit of other people's generosity. He wanted to laugh and lay his head in one of their laps. The other two became subdued.

Ashley rose suddenly. 'Excuse me. If you don't mind, I'll just take a little walk.'

They watched her stalk off down the rough track through the vineyard. She disappeared from view. Then Harry said, 'Is it safe?'

'Of course,' said Claudia. 'It will not be completely dark for another half an hour or so.'

Harry let his knee drift a little until it rested against Claudia's. He closed his eyes. The night lay ahead of them, like a gorgeous mystery.

'She is unhappy,' said Claudia.

Harry opened his eyes again. 'Yes.'

'Why?'

'She is unhappy because she is thinking about her lover in America and how he betrayed her ...' (Where else could he say a thing like this with a straight face? Only in Italy.) 'Tomorrow is the anniversary of the day he left her.'

124

'You and Ashley – you are not lovers?'

Harry shook his head. He'd met Ashley at a party in Rome about a year ago. They'd started talking about books and ended up talking all night. At dawn they'd gone walking along the banks of the Tiber and as the sun rose he'd tried to kiss her. That was when she told him about Brad. She told him the whole story. Every detail. 'He's both extremely ambitious and very weak,' she'd said. 'But I forgive him. He is my life.'

Harry passed the joint back to Claudia. 'We're just good friends.' Clouds of midges swarmed in the thickening yellow light. In the distance a church bell chimed and Harry thought unwillingly of all those people in Bologna who'd begun their day yesterday thinking it would be like any other, heading off to the station to catch a train. No warning. No logic. And for those who'd survived, how did you carry on living once you'd understood the scale of your own insignificance?

Claudia fussed some ash off the knee of her trousers. 'You didn't explain to me how this lover betrayed her, Harry.'

'Where to begin,' he sighed. But of course he knew. This was a story he'd heard so many times by now that in his own mind it had acquired the weight and texture of myth.

Brad and Ashley, he explained, had fallen in love some four years earlier at their exclusive East Coast boarding school. They soon became inseparable, doing their homework together in the oak-panelled library, walking hand in hand across the rolling green lawns, writing to each other every day when they were parted for 'vacations', as Ashley called them, until in their senior year of high school, tragedy struck. They had applied to all the same colleges, but when at last their acceptance letters arrived they found that only Brad had an offer from Harvard, while Ashley (but not Brad) had a place at Yale. Devastating. Still, they picked themselves up and made promises, as lovers do, to write and to be faithful and they believed that their love would survive the separation.

For some reason Claudia blushed violently at this point. Harry pretended not to notice.

'But around the same time this good-ol'-boy friend of the family showed up and decided to take Brad under his wing: show him how to get into politics. He introduced Brad to various useful people; he fixed him up with a summer internship in Washington, working for a Congressman. He opened Brad's eyes to the importance of choosing the right friends and, most important of all, having the right kind of woman at your side.' Harry gave Claudia a meaningful glance. 'The snake had entered the garden of Eden. Can you see Ashley pressing flesh at a fundraiser? Or schmoozing party donors?'

Claudia twisted her mouth. 'What happened? Tell me, Harry.'

Everything went along as usual until the night of their senior prom, Harry explained. It should have been the most romantic night of their gilded young lives, but Brad was in a sombre mood. While the rest of the class of '79 danced and drank and puked in the bushes, Brad asked Ashley to take a walk with him. They strolled hand in hand and he told her he would always treasure the memory of their time together, that she was a remarkable person, incredibly special. Then he spoke about his family and the expectations they had for him. He used words like "tradition" and "honour" and "public service". And then at last he told her that although it broke his heart, he had to confess that he'd begun to have feelings for the daughter of the Democratic Congressional Campaign Committee Chairman. He fell on his knees, heaving with loud, ugly sobs, and asked Ashley to forgive him and to set him free.

'*Che stronzo*,' said Claudia under her breath. What a shit.

'You said it.' Harry stretched his legs. 'All this happened at the beginning of last summer, which was a particularly

126

warm and lovely season. So whenever the sun shines and the days are long as they are right now, Ashley thinks of Brad and it's like a knife in her heart. And she cries easily, and wants to call him up, which is why we're taking this trip.'

'Politicians,' Claudia muttered. 'All of them are shits. Politicians and businessmen – all shits.'

'Ashley's father is a businessman.'

'Rich?'

'As a small country.'

Claudia gave a click of disgust. Harry laughed. 'I thought your father was also a businessman of a kind?'

'My father is also a shit,' said Claudia.

Harry ducked his head respectfully.

Ashley returned from her walk. She sat down and looked expectantly at Harry. Claudia, too, seemed to be waiting. Harry sighed and said, without moving his knee away, 'I suppose we should think of going soon.'

Claudia said nothing.

'Tell me, Claudia, do you know of a good *pensione* near here?'

'Eh?' said Claudia. 'You have no hotel? At this hour! Are you crazy?'

'Come on now,' said Harry, 'surely they don't close their doors till about eleven or twelve?'

'This is the tourist season,' Claudia said scornfully. 'Florence is full.'

There was a flat silence. Harry allowed himself to look crestfallen and foolish.

Claudia stood up and folded her arms. 'OK. There is nothing else to do. You will have to stay here,' she snapped.

'So kind of you, Claudia. Thank you, thank you,' Ashley mumbled through her cigarette.

'Are you sure now?' said Harry.

'Do I seem different to you?'

It was properly dark now. Claudia and Harry sat side

127

by side on the edge of the veranda sharing a final joint. Ashley had made her excuses and gone to bed in the spare room.

'In what way different?' Harry murmured.

'From the time we met before. In the mountains.'

Harry looked at Claudia in the reflected light of the house. He could just about make out her emphatic brows, her long nose, her heavy-lidded eyes. He could see the glow of Florence behind her through the trees.

'I mean in myself,' she said. 'As a person.'

'Ah, yes,' said Harry, though he had no idea really. 'Perhaps you do seem a little more serious. More mature.' He heard the briefest sigh of satisfaction.

'Since I met you last I have changed my life, Harry. I have fallen in love. I have been in prison.'

'Prison?!' Harry was genuinely surprised.

'Sssst!' she hissed. 'I was at a demonstration. There was some trouble and a whole group of us became arrested. If my parents find out they would kill me. First only Giovanna knew. She had to come and get me out of there. *O Dio!*' Claudia shivered and pulled the cardigan even closer about her. 'It was the worst night of my life.'

'Just the one night?'

'Any more and I would have suicided myself,' Claudia said.

'I see,' said Harry.

'My mother is an artist, a beautiful free spirit,' Claudia said. 'But in such things she is super-conservative. She would be worried for my reputation, my future. You know?'

Harry nodded. He thought of his own mother who, if you admired anything in the house, would tell you what she'd paid for it, and his father who'd eaten the same brand of breakfast cereal for thirty years. What would they say if they could see him now sitting here beside a Gucci princess, looking at the lights of Florence? Would they be impressed? Probably not. He remembered the slightly sorrowful expression that crept into their eyes when they looked at him these days. Harry, love, they'd say, where is all this leading? When are you going to get yourself a proper job?

'Not so long ago, I was the same,' Claudia went on. 'When I met you first at Christmastime, I was a child. I thought only of myself, my own small pleasures and problems. I was ignorant and spoiled. But my eyes have been opened, now. I feel a responsibility to join with others who fight for justice in our country. A day like yesterday – that bomb in the station – it makes me so convinced. This is a war, Harry, and I must play my part.'

'No one's claimed responsibility for the bomb yet.'

'Come on! It's obvious, no?' Claudia said scornfully. 'Bologna is a communist city. And think about where they left the bomb – in the 2nd class waiting room. It can only be *fascisti*.'

Harry nodded uncertainly.

She ground out the last of the joint against the step and flicked it away into the vineyard. 'Sometimes it feels heavy, this responsibility. But then my friend explains to me that if you study Marx, you see that what we struggle for now is inevitable. People like us, we are not creating this change, we are only helping it to come more quickly.'

Again he nodded. 'Right.'

'We are only servants of history.'

You too? Harry thought. You – with all your advantages – also dream of being a waitress?

In the middle of the night, Harry woke with a start. It took him a minute or two to remember where he was. He lay in the unfamiliar bed, listening. He could hear the low murmur of a woman's voice in the room next door, rising and falling, waiting, then beginning again. Digging back into his dream he recovered the sound of a phone ringing. That arsehole Brad! Ashley must have broken down and called him, then got him to call her back. Harry swung his legs over the edge of the bed and felt for his trousers on the rug. Ashley needed saving from herself.

But when he stepped into the sitting room he saw not Ashley but Claudia. She was sitting on the floor beside the phone on the coffee table. The receiver was back in its cradle but only just. She looked up at him with a strange expression.

'Is something wrong?' Harry asked.

'You should go back to bed,' said Claudia. 'I was just talking to a friend.'

'At three in the morning?'

'He is busy. He must ring me when he can.'

'Wow,' said Harry, 'he must be unbelievably busy.'

Claudia shrugged. She picked up the lit cigarette from the ashtray in front of her, then she looked beyond him and her face contorted. Ashley had appeared in the doorway of the spare room. She was barefoot and wearing a knee-length flannel shirt. With her dark hair spiralling around her head she looked like a girlish Struwwelpeter.

'I hate to ask, Claudia, but could I bum a cigarette? I can't find mine right now.'

With a kind of choking sound, Claudia rose and thrust the whole packet at Ashley. 'Take them all.'

Ashley looked embarrassed. 'No, I ...'

'It's OK. I have more,' and then, under her breath: 'O Madonna, O Dio. What must I do? I don't know. I don't know. *Mannaggia alla miseria*. Harry, please, I have to talk to you. Alone.'

Ashley retreated into the spare room again. Harry went and crouched beside Claudia. 'What's the matter?' He put an arm around her. He could feel her trembling. He smiled. He felt manly and useful and kind. 'Tell me. It's OK,' he murmured. 'You can tell me.'

Claudia shrugged him off. 'I'm sorry. I cannot explain this, Harry, but you have to go. You have to take her away from here. It's not safe any longer.'

Harry stopped smiling. He rose to his feet. 'Who was

that on the phone?'

Claudia clenched and unclenched the hand lying in her lap. Harry noticed how the nicotine had stained the inside of her fingers, spoiling her skin.

'He is a very clever person,' she said softly. 'I cannot see him often because he is in hiding. He is doing important work. He calls me when he can. It has taken me a long time to understand what he does, Harry. To people like my mother and father it would seem like crime and destruction, but out of his actions will come something better. Especially for people like Giovanna and Enzo who have had nothing for so long. It will be a new Italy, Harry. Soon. It must come.'

'Must it?' said Harry faintly.

Claudia began to cry again, although it seemed to Harry that part of her was enjoying the whole thing.

'Tonight he called, just to speak with me a little. He asked me what I was doing. It was just conversation. I told him about you and Ashley arriving with no hotel – a handsome Englishman, I said, and an untidy American girl. He asked me your names. I thought nothing about it. I was just telling him news from here. But he knew Ashley's name. He said her father is very rich. Then he asked me did anybody else know that you were here? And I said probably not. *O Dio!* I am sure he would not hurt her. It would only be for the money. But sometimes these things go wrong. And just now, when I saw her there in the door – Oh Harry! She is not my enemy. She is my age. She loves a man she cannot be with. She would be as afraid as I was in that prison that night. How can that be right, Harry?'

Harry couldn't help thinking of the newspaper pictures of the last kidnap victim they'd found – too late – curled up in the boot of a car like a child taking a nap. He wanted to say something to Claudia but he found himself standing up instead, moving towards the door. Claudia was a mess of tears again. '*Mi scusi*, Harry, *Mi scusi*, but you must go. Please.'

Ashley insisted on kissing Claudia goodbye. Harry watched them embrace on the veranda: two neglected little rich girls. Then Ashley climbed into the car and Claudia ran inside the house, hiding her face.

Harry let the Fiat roll down the long gravel drive without lights, just in case there were people watching from a distance. He coasted out onto on the main road and only then did he turn the key in the ignition. The car leapt at the tarmac like an animal.

When the house on the hill was far behind them, Harry let out a juddering breath. 'Jee-sus! That was close. You OK, Ashley?'

Ashley sat perfectly still in the seat beside him. 'Yes.'

She looked like one of those inscrutable early-Renaissance portraits, he thought, but without their steadiness or weight.

'What are you thinking about?'

'Weakness.'

'??'

'People equate emotion with weakness. Your friend back there thought it was a weakness on her part to feel pity and let us go. And Brad, when he choked off every emotion he'd ever felt and broke up with me on the night of the prom, he thought he was being strong. Funny, isn't it? It's the same thing.'

Harry pressed a little harder on the accelerator. His body was slick with sweat, his hands still trembling. Once or twice another car roared past them in the opposite direction and each time Harry wondered with a leap of fear if that was Claudia's man.

I could have got shot back there, he thought, or bundled into the boot of a car. And for what? Cadging a meal in the wrong house, driving around in a borrowed car with someone else's ex-girlfriend, loitering in a country that will never be mine. Something rose in his throat, a wave of nausea – as if he'd been overeating, gorging on too much rich food. The servants of history! What a joke.

Aloud he said, 'Tomorrow we need to go back, OK? I know I said a week, but I've changed my mind. There are things I need to do. OK?'

He took his eyes off the road for a moment. Ashley's head was tipped back, her eyes closed, lips parted, her breathing slow and steady. Harry gritted his teeth. It didn't seem to make much difference: awake or asleep, she saw mostly the back of her own eyelids anyway.

He didn't remember taking a turning but he must have done because the road began to narrow until it was no longer a main thoroughfare but an unpaved track without streetlights or visible signs of habitation. For a long while there was nothing but the close-up blur of earth unrolling before them, yard by yard. And then he saw it in the rear-view mirror: headlights, another car. It was a long way off but travelling fast because every time he looked the lights were bigger. Harry gripped the wheel. For a while he tried to push the Fiat to go faster. They bounced and juddered over the rough track, but still the lights in the mirror grew. The other car was gaining on them.

He thought about opening the door and simply flinging himself into the darkness, but in the end he decided to stop. Sometimes you had to give people a little bit of power over you. Sometimes you had to pretend to be weak so that they could feel they had a choice. Harry turned off the engine and swung around in his seat to face whatever was coming down the track. Beside him, Ashley slept.

Five to five on a Friday morning and Hazel lay in bed, waiting to be woken. It was at quiet times like this that the town seemed to press in on her most, hard and unforgiving. Hazel kept her eyes shut and dived back into her dream where Richard Burton and Elizabeth Taylor were wandering the streets, as they so often did.

Richard Burton wore one of those tweedy jackets with his shirt collar open and a faint shade of stubble on his face. He was drunk – not bloated with beer like the local men, but high-class drunk, with a breath that would burn pure blue if you lit a match. Elizabeth Taylor slouched in a low-cut dress and simple woollen coat, and the two of them wove along together, matching their steps, pulling close and then apart again like gum. You could see they were crazy about each other.

Brando sighed and swam towards Hazel in the bed. Hazel turned away.

In the dream, Richard Burton and Elizabeth Taylor had passed the old Bingo hall by now. They turned the corner by the boarded-up shoe shop, went along by the Blind Centre, then past number ten, then number twelve. They'd been walking and arguing all night and you could tell they were getting tired. They wanted to stop in somewhere and just sit a while. Let them come here, Hazel willed. Let them choose our house. Let them knock our door. Let them see me – just this once. Brando moved again, reaching up to put an arm around her neck.

'I's awake now, Hazel,' he murmured in his high baby voice.

'Gerroff!' she muttered. But the dream was already lost. She sat up and threw off the covers. 'I was *sleeping*!'

His face began to crumple.

She leaned in and kissed him quickly. 'Sorry Brando. Sorry boy.'

'Brando?' the vicar had said when her mother had dragged her down to the church to see about a christening. 'Are you sure you're not thinking of Bran? A lovely old Celtic name – or perhaps Brandon as in "from the beacon hill"?'

'No,' said Hazel. 'I'm thinking of Brando as in Marlon Brando.'

'I see,' said the vicar stiffly. But at least he made no remarks about adultery or fatherless children – not to her face anyway.

By seven o'clock Hazel and Brando were up and dressed. It didn't take long because they hadn't got very undressed the night before. They were fugitives from habit; they were bandits hiding out in this small-town two-up two-down. By 7.10 they were down at the kitchen table eating breakfast while Hazel's mother read the paper.

'Want a bickie,' said Brando.

'No,' said Hazel. 'Eat your toast.'

'Oh, I don't believe it, another disabled person murdered in Cardiff. In their own home, Hazel!'

Hazel made a face of stone.

Brando licked the jam off his toast. It went all over his chin and some strayed up into his hair. 'More, Hazel. Want more stuff on my toast.'

'No,' said Hazel, automatically.

'Can't say no, Hazel. Can't say no!'

'You just don't know who you can trust these days, do you?'

Hazel looked away. There was something too big and warm about her mother for the space they had. It hadn't always been like that. She had memories from her childhood of her mother laughing and teasing and full of fun. But somewhere along the line things had got stuck and twisted backwards into this kind of second-hand blood lust, this passion for other people's suffering. 'Oh my, oh Hazel. Listen to this …'

136

Out in the street Hazel could hear Linda The Milk talking to Melanie next door, clattering the empties.

'... little boy wandered away from his mum in a shopping centre. She turned her back for two seconds in the grocers and next thing he was gone ... there's pictures of him here on the security cameras ... "police fears for his safety are growing". Just a kiddie – not much older than Maggie's boy. Who would do such a thing, eh?'

For some reason Hazel thought about the way she used to wake up at night as a child, afraid that her mother would be dead or gone in the morning. She saw the memory like a piece of film, quite disconnected from herself as she was now: a small child sweating in the dark, holding onto her knees and trying to see the edges of the room, Maggie sleeping softly in the other bed.

'London this is, Hazel ...'

Hazel snapped off the picture and made herself think of London instead. She'd been there once when Maggie was a student. The thing she remembered most clearly was the house where Maggie had lived: bare floorboards and two kitchens, one on the ground floor, another on the floor above. That was interesting – odd.

'Think of the poor *mother*, Hazel.'

'Uh.'

'*Think* what she must be *going* through.'

Hazel had a great lurching feeling in her stomach. There was so much pain in the world. It was unbelievable the amount of suffering they lived with all around them. But she couldn't bear the way her mother sat sucking at the horror of it every day, like a maggot feeding on an endless sore. It drove her crazy

'Want more stuff on, Hazel,' said Brando again.

'No, you've had enough.'

'Can't say no, Hazel,' said Brando earnestly, putting his face up to hers. 'Policeman says: can't say no, Hazel.'

She looked at him: hair standing straight up from his face, a streak of green magic-marker next to one ear, a few

137

strawberry stains from yesterday's tea at the other. She felt a lurch of love.

'I wish you'd get him to call you Mum,' said her mother. 'Children need boundaries.'

After breakfast they went out to the park. Brando couldn't believe his luck. Most days they spent on the sofa watching old films on TV but today Hazel wanted to be away from all the last-minute preparations for Maggie's visit.

They went to the pond to watch the ducks and the greedy carp fighting for bread. They looked for ants. They played chase and Batman and Robin in the herb garden, and skidded up and down the gravel path by the bandstand. But Hazel's heart wasn't in any of it. And even in the park they weren't safe.

'Morning Hazel!' called Mrs Thomas, as they passed the bench by the monkey-puzzle tree. 'Saw your mother just now, over in Iceland.'

'Yeah?' said Hazel. 'Did she have the huskies with her?'

Mrs Thomas was a bit deaf so she just carried on smiling. 'I expect she was getting a nice bit of chicken for when your sister and her family come, then?'

That knocked all the joke out of Hazel. 'I suppose.'

'I expect she's really been looking forward, then, hasn't she, your mam?' Mrs Thomas showed her crooked teeth again, all gleaming in the sun, greedy for a scrap of someone else's happiness. On another day Hazel would have stopped to talk a bit, because Mrs Thomas was all right really, one of the few who had never been funny about Brando, but today she had no patience for it.

'Yeah well, better be heading back.' Hazel gave a tug at Brando's hand so that he whined. 'Ta-ra then Mrs T.'

'Mustn't keep you, Hazel,' said Mrs Thomas bravely. 'All the best to your sister, mind.'

What else? said Hazel under her breath: all the best and nothing but.

On the way back Brando grew complaining and over-tired. She had to carry him for the last bit and as they turned into their road he fell asleep in her arms. Maggie and Boyd's car was parked outside the house.

Hazel let herself in as quietly as she could. The house was full. She felt as if she had to push against the air to get in through the door. A babble of voices came from the kitchen: Boyd laughing with her dad, the kid shrieking, Maggie and her mam clattering about with plates and cups. Then Boyd and her dad went out in the garden with the kid and the voices in the kitchen dropped to a low murmur.

'Is she still seeing him, do you think?' she heard Maggie ask.

It's amazing how much space a 'family' takes up, thought Hazel. Just one extra person and they use up twice as much space as they should. They probably don't even notice it themselves. They just flatten everything around them.

'Does he have any contact with Brando?'

'To tell you the truth Maggie, I don't know.' There was a little silence. 'He's back with his wife now of course.'

Hazel could imagine the look between them.

'And Hazel? Is she still watching all those old black and white films?'

'Day in and day out.'

Silence.

'I've tried, Mags, I really have. I say to her, "What about evening classes?" I say, "Look what an education did for Maggie!" I'd be happy to watch Brando for her, I really would ...'

'Hi-yah,' Hazel said loudly, stepping out into the middle of the room. Brando was like a sack of lead in her arms but she wouldn't let them see that. She just stood and smiled at them with all her might, her lip snarling up a little at one corner. Her mother looked mortified. Maggie acted like there was nothing wrong.

'Hazel,' she came up and kissed her sister and laid a

139

hand on the head of the sleeping child. 'You're looking just the same!'

'You've put on a bit of weight,' said Hazel, which was true enough.

Maggie smiled bravely.

'Better put Brando to bed then,' said Hazel.

'Maggie and Boyd and Rupert are in your room again,' her mother called as Hazel climbed the stairs, 'and you two are in with me in the back bedroom. Dad's on the sofa. All right?' (All the best and nothing but.)

On Sunday Brando woke at half past seven. This time Hazel was awake already. She found it hard to sleep in the same bed as her mother. She lay on the edge of the mattress, trying not to roll in and touch that scented flesh. She could barely remember the dream: just the faintest trace of Richard Burton's sulphurous eyes.

She missed Brando. She leaned over the edge and looked at where he lay on a little mattress on the floor.

'Hazel!' he whispered, stretching out his arms. He had a habit of whispering until he was properly awake. It was a nice thing. Hazel slipped down onto the floor and cuddled up next to him. He wriggled his toes with pleasure. He smelled of rancid oil and baby soap. He was so warm. Hazel breathed him in.

'Hazel.'

'Brando.'

She rubbed her nose against his. 'Good boy, Hazel,' Brando murmured sleepily.

In the afternoon she and Maggie went up to the park with the kids. They sat on a bench watching Brando and Rupert play.

'I notice you've got some more pictures up on your wall.'

'Yeah,' said Hazel, reaching for her cigarettes. She didn't trust this careless intimacy. This was Maggie's professional *how're-ya-feeling* voice.

'Richard Burton again, eh?'

'So?'

'You like him, don't you?'

Hazel shrugged. 'Maybe.'

Across the grass in the sandpit, Brando emptied his bucket and handed it to Rupert. Rupert seemed to be explaining something. Brando squatted down beside him, listening with a trusting look. Rupert was a nice-enough kid. It wasn't his fault. Perhaps it was just that she wasn't much interested in children apart from Brando.

'They seem to get along, don't they?' Maggie said, following the direction of her gaze.

'I suppose.'

'He's a lovely little lad, Brando.'

'Why wouldn't he be?'

Maggie raised an eyebrow but she didn't seem annoyed. It was the way she was trained, Hazel decided. Maggie was 'handling' her now – just like the crazy people she worked with.

'He looks a lot like you now. Much more than ...' Maggie stopped herself abruptly, '... much more than he did in the first year.'

Hazel drew on her cigarette. She was coiled tight as a spring inside. If Mags says anything more like this, she thought, if she so much as mentions Richard Burton – or John – I'll get up and walk away, real quick, just like I didn't hear.

'I saw him once, you know,' Maggie said in an oddly soft, almost dreamy voice. 'When I was first in London.'

Hazel felt almost sick. She didn't know that John had ever been to London. She tried to raise herself off the bench but somehow her knees wouldn't work.

'It's funny, that – you know, when you see a famous person in real life,' Maggie said in the same disconnected voice.

A famous person? What was she talking about?

141

'Years ago, this was. When I was still a student. I was walking through Covent Garden, all dressed up in this black silk dress with this beautiful little red and gold bolero jacket and my hair cut really short and this hat ...' Maggie paused for a moment and shook her head. 'The money I wasted on clothes in those days. You wouldn't believe it. Anyway, there I was, feeling really pleased with myself, and I felt this man watching me from the other side of the road. And it was Richard Burton.'

Hazel couldn't think of a single thing to say.

'They were making an advert,' said Maggie. 'They must have been on a break. The crew were fussing about with their equipment and he was standing off to one side in this white linen suit and a Panama hat. I had to really look, to make sure, you know, that he was who I thought he was. He wasn't at all embarrassed. He just smiled and gave me a little wave, like this,' Maggie moved her hand against the air in a little wiping motion. 'And then I walked on.'

There was a child on the far side of the park running with a kite. It swooped and failed three or four times, bumping along on its nose, then it caught on a thin ribbon of air and it began to climb, haltingly, behind the running figure.

'It must have been just before he died. I saw the ad on TV later and, if I remember it right, he was already dead when they showed it.'

Even this, thought Hazel, even this she takes away from me. Doesn't she have enough?

'You can always come and stay with us if ever you want to get away, you know that, don't you?'

Hazel jerked her head. 'What do you mean "get away"?' she said tightly.

Across the park, the kite bucked and dipped in the air above the child's head, caught in a cross-current of breezes. The child ran faster, dragging it on.

Maggie tilted her head. 'I can see that this arrangement has a lot going for it. Mam and Dad really dote on Brando.

And I can see that they depend on you a lot in a way, especially now that they're getting older.'

Hazel half turned to her sister in surprise. She'd always thought no one else noticed this.

'It's more you I'm thinking about, Hazel. This is such a small town. In London it wouldn't matter whose kid he was. Nobody would care.'

Neither of them moved for a bit. Hazel thought about London: evil pleasure city; city of houses with two kitchens. At the far side of the park the child came to the end of the fence and stopped in his tracks. The kite began to dip and dive its way to the ground, lodging in the mud like a stricken bird. It didn't seem to occur to him that he could turn around and run back.

'Time to go,' said Hazel briskly, as if she had a rigid schedule to her days. 'Brando needs his tea.'

Maggie got up and followed meekly. Even that was irritating. It costs her nothing to do what I say, thought Hazel.

In the early half-light of Monday morning, Hazel slipped out of her mother's bed and onto the mattress where Brando lay. She closed her eyes and went back to sleep almost at once. This time the dream came easily. She was out in the streets with Richard Burton and Elizabeth Taylor again, listening to the clack of Elizabeth's beautiful shoes on the grey paving stones. Then she was back inside the house, standing in the hallway, listening to their approach. They were sweeping towards her. They were outside the door. They rapped the knocker and she put out her hand to lift the latch and she thought she would burst with the beating of her heart. And she put out her hand ... And she put out her hand ...

Hazel sat up suddenly so that Brando tumbled off her in a heap.

'Wakey-wakey Brando!'

Brando looked surprised.

'Time to get up,' said Hazel fiercely.

They went down to eat breakfast with Maggie, Boyd and Richard who were leaving early so that they could miss the traffic on the way back to London. Mam fussed about in the kitchen. Dad went off to the bus station to get the early morning papers: tabloids for the house, qualities for Maggie and Boyd to take back in the car.

'Sad business in here today,' he said, coming back into the room with a rush of cold air. 'Found his body last night. That little chap in London.'

Mam's eyes were black caverns of despair. She stood looking out at her family. 'Oh no!'

Hazel jerked her head away.

'Poor little mite.' Mam leaned over the picture of the smiling face on the front page, one hand clutching the dressing gown to her breast. 'Such wickedness. Poor lamb. No older than our Rupert. What chance ...? Innocent defenceless little ...'

Brando crawled up onto Hazel's lap and she buried her face in his hair. She had to open her mouth to get her breath. She didn't want to be like her mother. But somehow the tears came anyway, flooding up from some well-hidden dam inside her.

Maggie got up and put her arms around her mother.

'You will be careful won't you love? You will take care of Rupert won't you? You will make sure he's never alone or ...'

'Don't worry Mam. We're fine,' and Maggie rocked her mother against her like a child.

Boyd and Dad packed the car and Mam took Rupert with her for a last check in the upstairs rooms for forgotten toys and stray socks.

'You'll think about what we talked about yesterday, won't you?' said Maggie. 'About visiting?'

Hazel hesitated.

'Don't be put off by that news story,' Maggie said

quickly. 'London's no more dangerous than anywhere else. It could have happened anywhere.'

Hazel thought of Maggie being in London when she was young, and Richard Burton watching her. She remembered why she had followed Maggie around everywhere once and wanted to be like her. Perhaps I will do it, thought Hazel. She felt a sudden spurt of energy, as if a door opened a little bit inside her head again. She thought how light and easy she would feel in a place where nobody knew her: away from John and his wife and the watching streets.

'Maybe,' she said, grinning.

'Do it!' whispered Maggie, squeezing her hand. 'Come soon.'

As the car disappeared around the corner, Hazel let her mother put an arm about her. 'They'll be back in a couple of months,' she said lamely. She allowed herself to be hugged.

Mam shook her head. 'You never stop worrying about your children whatever age they are. You'll understand how I feel one day, Hazel. You're a mother yourself now.'

'Yes,' said Hazel. They stood for a moment looking out at the road, then her mother turned slowly back to the house. One day I will be like that, thought Hazel, and Brando will be like Maggie: driving away to somewhere else.

Brando dropped down on his haunches on the front step, his hands clutched across his stomach.

'Ants,' he said, seriously.

'Uh huh,' said Hazel.

She could feel the very small flash of will to escape flickering out. Maggie would think that it was because of John but it wasn't. She didn't even think about John that much any more. It was more that she felt she wouldn't belong anywhere else but here. She'd overheard the vicar saying once: 'If they don't leave the Valleys by the time they're eighteen, they never get away'. Perhaps there was something in that.

Richard Burton was leaning against the Santoris' house across the street, smoking. 'Ah, come on now, Hazel,' he said in his half-wheedling, half-fighting tone. 'It's not such a bad old town, is it now?' Hazel ignored him. She didn't need Richard Burton butting in on things right now.

The parking-meter man was working his way down the street (it was residents only now). At the other end of the street, Mrs Collins and Mrs Edwards slowed to get a good look at what was going on. Brando was lying on his stomach on the pavement saying, 'Where's my ant Hazel? Where's it gone?'

Mrs Collins and Mrs Edwards said something to each other now and shook their heads. Hazel stepped out and gave them her fighting look, which got rid of them quick enough.

'So you made a mistake,' said Richard Burton, not understanding her train of thought.

'I did not!' Hazel snapped.

'So we all make mistakes. Sometimes the mistakes are the best part. So we go back and make them again. And again.' Richard Burton tossed his fag-end into the gutter and glanced up at the upstairs front bedroom where old Mrs Santori used to sleep before they took her off to the home. Elizabeth Taylor was standing by the window in her wedding dress, looking beautiful and pretending not to know it. Richard Burton winked at Hazel. 'That's life, isn't it though, Hazel? You can travel far and wide and see nothing, and you can stay at home and see it all. Isn't that so?'

In the upstairs room, behind the net curtains, Elizabeth Taylor spun around a few times, just for fun. And in the street Brando cried out in triumph, '*There's* it! Look, Hazel! My ant!'

From deep inside the house Hazel could hear her mother calling them. She knew there'd be a fresh pot of tea on the table by now, her father dozing in the easy chair and Mam rustling at the pages of the day's news. She could always go in and put the TV on for a bit. They might be showing a thirties comedy or a forties B-movie. It would pass the time. Hazel glanced back at the house, then out to the road.

'Look Hazel,' Brando said again.

And Hazel looked. There was Brando with his arm outstretched, showing her the ant in the cup of his palm, head tipped back so that the fringe fell away from his head in waves, feet planted squarely on the pavement – all flesh and blood and colour and not going anywhere yet. So much time she'd wasted on Richard Burton and Elizabeth Taylor and all those other people who didn't belong to her when everything she needed was right in front of her. She took Brando's sticky hand.

'Let's get your coat, boy.'

'Why, Hazel?'

'Because we're going up the park.'

'Who with, Hazel?'

'Just you and me, boy. Just you and me.'

They had driven to Wales from London late the night before. Even before they set out they were exhausted. All the way through the business of leaving their house – locking windows, switching off lights, carrying the bags and the howling baby out to the car – they had argued, bitterly, furiously, until they lost all notion of what it was they wanted from one another and only a sense of miserable, injured, short-changed grievance remained. Most of the five-hour drive passed in silence.

The weather seemed to pick up their mood and magnify it. Rain battered the windscreen. Gusts of wind shook the car. Sarah was afraid they would overturn and be thrown into the whirling, sticky blackness. The usual signs flashed by: Hungerford, Maidenhead, Bristol, Cardiff. Hard to believe such places still existed when they were in the middle of such darkness. For long stretches there were no lights along the motorway and then it felt as if the road itself had been abolished. They could have been driving under the sea or stalled, just a set of headlights drilling into oblivion. And through it all the poor baby slept in his cot on the backseat, unaware that his world was coming undone.

Now and then the car wavered in its lane. Sarah felt John's strength falter and she understood the effort it took to keep the three of them on this road. She wondered, not for the first time, whether this was the cost of her choice. She was forty-three and he fifty – far too old to be having babies.

People found it bizarre that they should become parents now, after fifteen years of marriage. Why wait so long? they'd say, or: whatever for? – depending on their attitude to children. 'It was an accident,' she'd say. 'We thought we couldn't.'

Most people laughed at that but some looked

disappointed, as if they wished she'd invented a prettier story. Still, it was the truth.

By the time they reached his mother's place it was one in the morning and the town was shuttered up for sleep, with only a few late-night stragglers stumbling home. Ann was at the door as soon as she heard their car, greedy arms outstretched.

Sarah and John put on a show of being on speaking terms, but Ann wasn't interested in them. 'Give him to me,' she crooned. 'The babe, the babe. Let me hold him. Come to me, my precious.'

The next day was freezing but bright, rinsed clean by the storm. To Sarah's relief, her mother-in-law set out early with one of the neighbours to be sure of getting good seats in church. Sarah and John got ready in silence. When it was time to leave the house John went ahead without a backward glance, leaving Sarah to follow with the pram. There was no traffic so they walked in the middle of the road. Fifteen years. His face was so familiar to her that she could hardly even see him, and yet lately he'd become a stranger.

She had given up her job when she discovered she was pregnant. She wanted to spend the first year with the child and they could manage on one salary for a while, but at times like this she felt she'd made a terrible mistake. She had made herself dependent just as John became undependable. She had fallen off the map. There were moments of great joy, but she was always responding, always governed by the machine-gun tattoo of the child's needs or John's moods, supplying whatever seemed to be required. Now. Now. Now. Some days she felt that 'accident' was the most accurate description of what had happened to them and that everything she'd ever known and valued had been consumed in the wreckage.

A pigeon flapped by overhead and the baby gave a

wordless exclamation of pleasure. That was new. She smiled down at him, admiring the curve of his head, the kiss-curl on his brow, those fat, perfect little hands fiddling with the tassels of his blanket. Who will he become, she wondered? I wish he could tell me.

She leaned in to straighten the neck of his christening gown. He caught a hank of her hair and tugged it like a bell-pull. She laughed. The feeling of dread inside her lifted a little. It was 9.15 a.m. They had fifteen minutes before the start of the service.

She walked on.

Each street was much like the next, rows of two-up, two-down houses, mostly pebble-dashed and double-glazed. Outside Mitzi's Hair Salon John had paused, waiting for her to catch up, though he still kept his back turned. An elderly man with a terrier stopped to talk to him. Sarah slowed her pace, hoping that the man would be gone before she got there. She wasn't in the mood for small talk.

But John turned and beckoned to her, beaming, as if no cross word had ever passed between them. 'Sarah, come and say hullo. This is Rhydian. Rhydian, this is my wife. And this ...' John looked down at the pram with a faintly surprised expression. '...this is my son.'

They all stood and gazed at the child. How could such a gleaming creature have sprung from two such worn and bitter bodies?

'I've known Rhydian all my life,' John said. 'I remember during the miners' strike, we'd be out in front of Woolworths collecting for them. Isn't that right, Rhydian?'

'Aye.' The old man nodded.

'That's, what, twenty years ago, now?'

'Thirty, more like,' said Rhydian, wheezing. 'You were still a bit wet behind the ears back then.'

John shook his head. 'Terrible. All those pits closed in the end, just like we said.'

'Aye,' said Rhydian. 'And Woolworths.'

The baby had begun to fuss and wriggle under his blankets.

'We need to get a move on, John,' Sarah whispered. To Rhydian she explained that Ann was keeping seats for them in the church. She nodded down at the child. 'He's being christened today.'

'Mustn't keep you, then,' said Rhydian, patting John on one shoulder. 'Give my best to your mother.'

They walked on. Soon the high street was in view. Groups of mostly elderly people in their best clothes were making their way up the hill towards the church. But John was looking in the opposite direction, down a side road.

'When I was ten I fell off my bike over there,' he said. 'Skinned my leg all the way from the ankle to the knee. And down this road, when I was older, sixteen or seventeen, I remember I persuaded this boy to let me try his motorbike. But he didn't tell me how to stop. I had to crash into a wall.' The meeting with Rhydian seemed to have tipped him back into the past. 'When I went up to the grammar school, I used to travel with a boy who lived on the left, there, Gareth Mason.'

Sarah chewed her thumbnail. Somehow she had to get him to hurry up without triggering a row. Ann would be counting the seconds by now, eyes fixed on the door at the back of the church.

'Gareth Mason, eh?' She forced a smile.

'Yes, he lived along there at number twelve. He was abroad for years, working for one of the big oil companies, but he's been ill. My mother was telling me he's moved back home to recuperate.'

Sarah kept the smile going, though on the inside she was raging: that she should be forced to behave like an air hostess with her own husband, and worst of all, that John seemed to prefer this fake, grinning persona to her real self.

'Tell you what,' he was saying, 'I'm just going to knock the door and see if Gareth's there. Just a quick hullo. We've got plenty of time.' He took the pram away from her and set off down the side street. Sarah followed, the soles of her good shoes slapping on the tarmac. What will we do after today, she wondered? The road keeps running into sand.

A gaunt-looking man answered the door. There was laughter and back-slapping, then to Sarah's dismay the two of them began to pull the pram into the house. Had John lost his mind? The service was about to begin. They had seven minutes to get to the church.

'A baby, eh?' said Gareth Mason, looking everywhere but at the child. He showed them into a warm, cluttered sitting room where a game of football played silently on TV. 'I'll make some tea, shall I?' He left the room.

'We don't have time for this!' Sarah hissed. She yanked the pram handles in her temper so that the baby gave a soft cry of protest.

John didn't seem to hear. He was kneeling on the floor, looking through Gareth Mason's vinyl collection, murmuring with pleasure at various albums he recognized.

Gareth came back and leaned in the doorway while he waited for the kettle to boil. 'They were up in the loft for years,' he said, nodding at the stack of albums. 'Mam never throws anything out.'

John pulled out a David Bowie album. 'Unbelievable, isn't it, to think he's gone?'

'Shocking,' said Gareth.

'He always looked so alive. So indestructible. Though mind you, he had a heart attack in the noughties, didn't he? He nearly died on stage.'

John began to read through the song titles under his breath. 'Changes. That's him in a nutshell, isn't it? He reinvented himself so many times. So many lives he lived.'

Gareth opened his mouth to say something, but the kettle whistled in the kitchen. He went out.

Sarah was lurching between panic and a white-hot fury. She began to turn the pram around towards the hall.

'John, your mother is sitting there in front of the whole congregation waiting for us. We have to go right NOW or we'll miss the start and she will never, ever forgive us.'

John had pulled another record from its sleeve and was running one finger lightly around the outer rim.

'Did you hear me, John?'

'Let's not rush,' he murmured. 'It's just a normal church service to begin with. The christening bit isn't till the very end.' And then, almost inaudibly, 'There's something I need to tell you.'

'Oh.' She let her hands slip away from the pram. 'Right now?'

'There's never a good time, is there?'

A chill spread through her. I knew it, I knew it, I knew it. He's off. He's met someone who isn't constantly covered in baby sick, someone who finishes their sentences, who isn't always too tired for sex. She took a few faltering steps into the centre of the room, then retreated to the sofa so that when it came – the end of the road – she wouldn't have too far to fall.

'Go on.'

In the kitchen they could hear the ring of a spoon on china. Something metallic fell with a crash.

John put the record away. 'So,' he said. He scrubbed his mouth with the back of one hand. 'You remember I had that hospital appointment last year about the deafness on my right side? Remember? And I never heard back from them so I assumed ...'

This was not what she'd been expecting. Not at all.

John was still speaking. He was using words like: 'scan' and 'tumour'. Sarah wanted to respond but all she could manage was a strangled noise at the back of her throat.

'They put the result in the wrong pile, apparently, or they misfiled it, or lost it. Something. They should have called me in sooner,' he said. 'But anyway, they're on the case now. And it's not too late. It's a slow-growing one, apparently. So they're going to open up just here.' He indicated a place behind his ear. 'And whip it out.'

Sarah sank backwards into the sofa. Motes of dust tumbled in the stream of winter sunlight from the window behind her. She felt she might never get up again.

John came and sat beside her. 'You mustn't worry, Sarah.' He took her hand. 'The surgeon does these operations all the time. I googled him. He's world class.' He laughed. 'Funny, isn't it? All that time when you were pregnant, I was growing a tumour. Like a competition.'

She turned to him in a daze. How long is it, she wondered, since I've heard him laugh?

Gareth Mason came in clutching three mugs in his trembling, skeletal hands. 'I put milk in all of them,' he said. 'I wasn't sure.'

'Good man.' John's face was open and relaxed. You could see what he must have been like, Sarah thought, when he and Gareth Mason used to be friends.

Gareth gave Sarah her tea, then went over to the stack of records and fished out a cinnamon-coloured album. 'Remember this one, John? 1977, *Low*. Let me play you my favourite track.' He bent down and fiddled with the stereo.

'It'll be all right, Sarah,' John whispered. 'I promise.' And then, 'Sorry about the things I said last night. I didn't really mean any of it.'

'I love this one,' said Gareth, dropping the needle onto the disc.

There was a brief crackle like bacon in a pan, then David Bowie began to sing 'Always Crashing in the Same Car'. Gareth Mason hummed along and John drank his tea and the baby rubbed his ear and grew sweaty and fell asleep. And Sarah closed her eyes and went hurtling into the welter of possibilities ahead, hoping that John would be right, that they would be lucky – luckier than the miners, luckier than Woolworths, luckier, even, than David Bowie with all his many, many lives.

We see the signs in English and in Welsh as soon as we enter the hospital: 'Ward 19'. Underneath it says, also in English and in Welsh, 'Bereavement Office / *Swyddfa Profedigaeth*.' A clue. There probably isn't a ward 20.

Grace is huddled in an armchair beside her bed, looking smaller than ever. Her white hair, which has been thinning for a while, is reduced to a few wisps around her ears. The voice, though, is unchanged. 'I can't take much more of this, Vee,' she whispers as I hug her.

In another bed across the aisle lies a cadaverous woman, head tilted back on high piles of pillows, tearing every breath from the inside of an oxygen mask. In the bed directly opposite, a doll-like woman of ninety-two is being fed tea from a beaker. She looks as sweet as a dormouse with those enormous brown eyes, but Grace says she's horrible.

'I wish you didn't have to go,' Grace says at the end of visiting time. 'The nights are the worst.'

We talk about the possibility of bringing her back home. 'That would be lovely,' she says. But three days later, the consultant starts her on a low dose of morphine and she is moved from the open ward into one of the four enclosed cubicles. In hospital code that means: *not long to go.* Guiltily, reluctantly, we decide that we're not equipped to care for her at home, but from now on one of us will be with her all the time.

(i)

'I've come to sit with my mother-in-law,' I say when I arrive at eight on the first night, 'Mrs Edwards.'

The nurses look bemused. 'Oh, you mean Grace!' No one stands on ceremony in here: no knickers, no secrets, no surnames. 'In there, love.'

157

Grace is drowsy but seems pleased to see me.

At first I'm not sure of what to do. We've always had an easy relationship these twenty-five years, but this is new territory for both of us. I wipe her face and neck to cool her down. I help her to a drink of water. I settle into the armchair next to her bed, take her hand in mine and suddenly I relax. I become absorbed in the feeling of being next to her, listening to the rhythm of her breath, studying the patterns of purplish bruising on her arm. I've brought a book but I don't feel like reading. She drops off to sleep. I put my feet up on another chair, cover myself in a hospital blanket and, still holding her hand, slip into a doze. It's very peaceful. I'm glad to be there. Today is my forty-ninth birthday. I have known her more than half my life; it seems no time at all.

At around 10.30 p.m. they come and turn her and plug a new vial of antibiotics into the canula in her arm. An hour or so later Grace is awake and agitated. She is not herself any more.

'I've got to get up. Help me up.'

No, no, no. It's the middle of the night.

'I've *got* to get up. Got to stand.' She starts whipping off the sheets and trying to swing her skinny legs out of the bed. I scurry about trying to cover her up again, like some Victorian governess.

Perhaps we can move the bed up a bit, I say.

She fastens onto this idea. Yes. Up. 'UP, UP, UP! Get me up now! Now. *N-OW!*'

I try changing her position by moving the pillows. 'No!' she snaps. 'Leave it!' In the end, one of the nurses comes and shows me how to use the controls to raise the top part of the bed so that Grace is more or less in a sitting position.

'More,' she keeps saying: imperious, impossible to reason with – wilful as a child, consumed by the totality of what she wants. 'UP, UP, UP! Higher! Now. NOW.'

'That's enough, Grace. I can't take it any higher.' Any further and she'll tip right out of the bed.

'More. Up. Up. Higher.'

'You'll fall, Grace.'

She picks up the phrase and starts to weaves it into her anxious chant. 'I'm falling. I'm falling. Hold me! I'm falling!' Singing out in wild despair: 'Oh GOD!'

I reach in and embrace her. I put my best into it, everything I've got.

'Ow,' she says, in a smaller, more normal voice. 'You're hurting my neck.'

'Sorry, sorry.'

She starts talking about her arm. It's hurting. It's so painful. It's falling off. 'Oh it's AGONY. Oh GOD, my arm!'

I get the nurse back. She switches on the blasting overhead lights and we can see that the flesh around the canula is swollen and red; the needle has slipped out of the vein. The nurse disconnects the drip, and tells me they'll put in a call for one of the nurse practitioners to come and insert a new line. It must be very sore, she says sadly. They give Grace something for the pain and slowly she grows calmer. She slips into a doze.

When the nurse practitioner finally arrives in the early hours of the morning I tell her about 'up, up, up'. She nods as she searches for a vein on Grace's other arm. 'Fluid on the lungs,' she says. 'They get the feeling they're drowning. I know what I'd want if I was her.' How quickly all this is unravelling. Already we've begun to talk as if she wasn't there.

(ii)

The following night Grace wakes at 3 a.m., highly agitated, worse than before. 'I've got to get up, Vee. You've got to help me. I know I've got to get out of here. Please, Vee, *please*.' It's heart-breaking. 'Please, Vee.' She keeps repeating this over and over, clutching at my hand. 'You've got to help me, Vee. So difficult – I'm all muddled in my thinking. Please, Vee, PLEASE. I know I've got to get out of here.'

I feel so low and mean and two-faced. In a novel I would smuggle her out and we'd go for one last crazy midnight trip to the seaside or something. Except this isn't a novel. And I know – as she doesn't – that she probably isn't going to get out of here. 'A matter of days,' the cardiac specialist has said. 'Probably Friday,' says the ward consultant.

'You can't get up now, Grace. It's night-time.'

'You're not helping.'

'Everybody's sleeping, Grace.'

The nurse comes to try and help, takes her hand, leans in, listening. 'What do you want, Grace? Tell me.'

'I need shelter. Take me to my shelter. Take Grace to her shelter. I need you to take Grace to her shelter. I need you to –' She's hardly able to catch a breath, almost hiccuping.

'It's all right. I'm here,' I say.

Suddenly she's intensely warm. She turns to me, clutches at my arm, hugging it against her chest. 'I need my Vee. Where's Vee. I need my lovely Vee. I need her. Hold me. Keep me safe. I'm falling. Hold me together. We've got to keep it together. I'm so frightened. Hold me. Feel my heart.'

I lean in over the bed with both arms around her. The pressure of fear builds and builds.

'Feel my heart.'

I put my hand on her heart, feel its wild hammering. I thought it was supposed to be weak? It feels incredibly strong to me. Perhaps it will burst?

A flicker of lucidity. 'I'm finding this very difficult.'

She isn't ready. She isn't 'coming to terms' or 'at peace' or 'starting to accept' or anything remotely like that. She can feel life slipping away from her and she's fighting every step. She wants to live. It's terrible.

She switches. 'I need to talk. I need to talk about things I remember.'

The nurse leaves us.

Grace begins. She's back in early childhood, four, five, six years old. She talks about being in court. 'Got to say the right thing. Got to be quiet. Got to be good. I need a wee. Can't go now, have to wait. Didn't know it was going to be like this. But we've got to help them. What can we do? We've got no money to give them? How can we help them? They'll have to go. We can't help them. There's no work. I'm only six. No work for me. Got to say the right thing. Got to be a good girl.'

It sounds like an eviction, neighbours or friends perhaps. It's nothing I've ever heard her talk about before. It feels very real, like a long-buried secret coming out of hiding. She was a child during the Depression, a time before unemployment benefits or free healthcare or free secondary education – who knows what she saw or heard.

'He's carrying me up the stairs.'

I know she's talking about her father, now. He was a coal miner, a rough, sweet man; dead more than forty years.

'Where? In Castle Street?'

'Yes. He's carrying me up the stairs. He's pulling my side to get me to say the right thing.' Wincing with pain. 'He's pulling very hard. He's going to pull me through.'

Then, in a colder tone: 'You've got to apply the right verbs to me. Apply the right verbs. Many. A lot.' Sadly, 'She's always pushing me. She pushes too hard.' She's talking about her mother now: no warmth here. Her mother was a hard woman. Doll, they called her. Pretty Doll.

Later, it's her father again. 'He's calling me. Can you hear him? You can hear him, too, can't you?' She stares ahead into the room. Her face is soft and open, very interested; now she's not at all afraid.

'What's he saying? "Gracie"?'

'Yes.'

'He always took care of you, didn't he?'

'Yes.'

'So many people have taken care of you, haven't they?

Your father, your mother. Paul. Paul always looked after you, didn't he?'

I suppose I'm feeding her her husband's name on purpose. I want to hear some reassuring declaration of love and longing: soon to be reunited. Wouldn't that be nice? But she looks vague. 'I can't remember,' she says. She and Paul were married for forty-four years. He gave up his job to look after her when she had her breakdown at thirty-six; he never worked again, was always poor, and still thought himself lucky to have her. All that seems to have gone missing. She talks about the present and the distant past, childhood; the vast long middle stretch of her life – marriage, motherhood – has vanished.

'Paul,' I say again.

'So many people,' she murmurs. 'I can't remember all their names.'

(iii)

People knock on the door for news when they see we're back at the house: the Sicilian neighbours, people from the church, old friends. Grace has a gift for friendship, always wonderfully accepting of other people. Back in the sixties she made friends with the only black family in the village and kept in touch long after they'd moved away. And I remember her saying how unfair it was that the woman across the road had a reputation for slovenliness: 'It's just that she doesn't like housework.'

One of the more annoying visitors is Beverly, the daughter of one of Grace's friends, who has fallen into the habit of parking outside Grace's house and putting a note in the window for the parking wardens: 'Visiting no. 9.' Beverly has rubbery lips and an imposing mop of brown curls. She'll call in to the house to ask if Grace wants anything from 'over town', then stride off to the high street to check Tesco, Aldi, Lidl, Iceland for dented tins, end-of-the-line reduced items, special offers, buy-one-get-one-free, any type of bargain. It's clearly a full-blown addiction, like gambling or crack. She talks of nothing else.

'What about her hair, though?' we used to say to Grace. 'Is it a wig?'

Shocked looks. 'No, no, of course not. Beverly used to be a hairdresser. She's got lovely hair.'

Beverly knocks every other day, ostensibly to ask how Grace is, but actually so that she can park outside the house. 'Want anything from Iceland?' she says, hair bouncing and trembling like a wild brown cloud.

(iv)

Then it's Friday, the day the consultant thought would be her last. By now Grace, too, is drinking from a plastic beaker, and the panic attacks have begun to spill over into the daylight hours. The lanky nurse on duty that night watches an early evening episode, blinking behind her glasses.

'She's frightened,' she says to me, in the corridor. 'It goes like this at the end with some people. She knows it's coming.'

This third night feels more wearing. The anxiety attacks are longer, more relentlessly repetitive. She keeps trying to get out of bed, calling, 'Treatment! I need treatment!' She's hurrying so much that at times she can't make real words, just spits out sounds with her tongue: 'Blea-uh, blea-uh, blea-uh.'

At some ridiculous level I find myself disapproving of her tenacity, as if it's a kind of greed, a lack of acceptance. I don't think I'd struggle this hard, not even at the age I am now. Perhaps I don't love life enough. Perhaps I'll feel differently when I get to eighty.

We slide into an endless conversation about making phone calls. 'Got to call Ann,' says Grace. Ann is a friend from childhood. 'Must talk to Ann. She will help me. I can trust Ann. Got to call ...'

163

'You can't call Ann now. It's night-time. She's sleeping.'

She accepts this for an instant. Then it starts all over again: 'Got to call Ann.'

I try to move us into a conversation. 'You were seven, weren't you, when Ann was born? People used to think you were sisters.'

'That's right. We used to go swimming.'

'That must have been lovely. Was Ann a good swimmer?'

Clearly this is an incredibly stupid question, almost not worthy of a reply. Long pause. 'No.'

'Ann's been calling every day for news about you. We'll bring the mobile into the hospital tomorrow and you can talk to her.'

'She's got a lovely voice, Ann. She always finds the right words for me. She'll know what to say. I can trust Ann.'

In the morning I go out to grab a cup of coffee. When I come back the day shift has arrived and the new nurse and auxiliary are just tucking her into clean sheets. They seem to have upset her. She's calling out very loudly: 'Why am I not being properly attended to?! Why have I just been left? Why am I not being properly treated! *Why* is nobody paying *attention* to me?!'

This imperious, newly demanding personality is startling after a lifetime of timidity. Where was she hiding these qualities? The deference to the doctors is still intact, though. You can see her gathering together the fragments of a social persona with enormous effort whenever a white coat appears.

'And how are you today, Grace?'

'Fine thank you, Doctor. Not too bad.'

To Ben she says, 'Mustn't get on the wrong side of the doctors.'

To John, her younger son, she says: 'It's just you and me, John. We've got to stick together.'

164

(v)

By the weekend Ben and I are taking it in turns to do the nights. On the Saturday night, Grace keeps going more or less constantly all night, and Ben ends up reading book reviews aloud just to short-circuit the anxious chatter. 'What a crazy idea to give old people drugs so they die tripping,' he says, somewhere between laughing and crying.

My brother-in-law John believes in the power of positive thinking. Every day as he drives over to visit Grace he pictures an empty space in the car park and there's always one there waiting for him. He says that when he sits with her in the hospital he imagines her healing inside. He reports certain improvements: there are days when she takes a couple of mouthfuls of cereal; she's drinking lots of water; she's started asking for tea; she's had a vitamin drink. He thinks her bruises are clearing up. He thinks her hair is starting to grow back. He starts talking about the possibility of a nursing home. Ben shakes his head. One evening he's out in the garden of his mother's house and he sees a huge dark bird passing overhead, a stork perhaps, great wings flapping. He feels it like an omen of tragedy: a great shadow stork, not bringing life but coming to take it away.

The truth is that none of us knows what's ahead. When we step back from the moment-by-moment business of being with her in the hospital, it feels as if we're locked in an ever-darkening tunnel. We don't know how to read what we see in front of us. We've never been here before. We have no maps. We are badly lost.

(vi)

On the Sunday night, Grace's skin is itching, driving her crazy. Her nails are sharp. She's drawn blood on her arms and legs and on her back, so I take over. The pretty young

English nurse on duty finds me standing beside the bed scratching my mother-in-law's head.

'Both sides!' Grace is saying. 'Scratch harder. Yes. That's it. Harder.'

The nurse laughs. 'That's how I was when I was in labour. "Stroke my faa-ace!"'

Later, when Grace starts chanting 'Up, up, UP' again, I go out to the nurses' station to see if there's anything they can give her for the anxiety. The nurse looks suddenly young and a bit frantic herself. 'Oh!' she says. Deferring to a more senior colleague: 'Can I give her more morphine?' Apparently not. Too much morphine can make people *more* rather than less anxious.

So I go back and get the washcloth. I wipe Grace's face, her neck, her arms, her back. I rub down under the collar of her nightdress, over her stomach, up into the folds under her breasts, behind her ears, in the hollow of her throat. 'That's *lov*-ely,' she murmurs. 'Ooooh yess. Lovely! Hmmm.' Over and over again I wipe her, rinsing out the cloth at intervals to make it cool. Then I dry her and put moisturizer on her skin, rubbing along her arms and down to her firm smooth back, and along her skinny, shiny-shinned legs, smoothing her, soothing her. By the time the nurse returns to offer more drugs, Grace is asleep. I feel an enormous sense of achievement, but also sadness for all the people who have no one to touch them like this.

I hold her hand while she sleeps. Outside it's August, a chilly summer's night. Away at the bottom of the hill, dogs are barking and snarling on the streets of the nearby housing estate. From where I'm sitting it's the sound of passion and impulse, the sound of life itself, and it seems ludicrously far away. I am buried in the timeless, aseasonal matrix of the hospital. Somewhere down the hall I can hear the silvery bing-bong of a blocked IVAC machine, and closer still, in this room, the swish and crackle as the air sighs in and out of the pneumatic mattress. Night shift, day shift, back again to the night. We are far away from the world. We are in the Valley. Deep in. How many more days like this?

(vii)

On Tuesday afternoon, Ben's cousin Megan brings an old friend to the hospital at visiting time. Lou has known Grace since they were girls; she was a bridesmaid at Grace and Paul's wedding. At first the visit goes well, but when Megan is out of the room, Grace starts flinging off the covers again, and Lou, probably embarrassed by Grace's lack of underwear, keeps trying to cover her up. In the tussle of blanket on, blanket off, on, off, on, off, Grace rips out the catheter, then the drip. It's hard to know whether it's accidental or not; she has tried to rip them out before.

The doctors decide to change her treatment plan to something called 'Clear Pathways'. They will continue to administer pain relief and sedatives but they are no longer treating any of her medical conditions, including the diabetes. There's no point in giving her insulin since she's not eating, but if her blood sugar drops they won't give glucose either. Clear Pathways.

By Tuesday night, her breathing is noticeably more laboured. Sometimes she closes her mouth and the breaths are dragged through her nose with enormous effort. Sometimes she breathes through her mouth and you hear the rattling of the fluid in her lungs. They tell us that they can put a tube down her throat to suction out the build-up but it's a painful procedure and the fluid will come back. No, we say. Clear Pathways.

On Wednesday morning, when I'm still there after the night, Elaine, the hospital priest comes. She's been several times over the weeks to give Grace Communion. Now she peers at the bed: 'It's very close,' she murmurs. 'You should tell her sons to come. They should hurry.' It's true that there is a new transparency to Grace's features. She looks peaceful. Her skin is soft and childlike. Her forehead is smooth.

'Would you like me to bless her?'

I nod. Increasingly, I have found myself reaching for religion when I'm with Grace, being glad of my Bible-saturated schooldays, not the belief but the ritual. I have sung hymns to her. We've recited the Lord's Prayer. When there's no sense to be had in conversation, you need the weight and power of old words: *Yea though I walk through the Valley of the Shadow of Death, yet will I fear no evil, for thou art with me.*

I call Ben and Ben calls John and they both come over. They stay with their mother for much of the day; Ben stays on for the night. This is it, I think. This will be the last night.

In the morning, Ben calls me from the hospital. He has spent the time talking to his mother, thanking her, telling her how much he loves her, telling her how beautiful she is.

'I know she heard me,' he says. 'I could tell by the way her breathing changed.'

The day wears on. I don't want to go in again. I have put down the burden and I don't want to pick it up again. I'm so tired. 'No one could possibly ask you to do any more than you've already done,' says Ben. 'Stay home if you want.' I *do* want. I am not going back. Never, ever again. I can't do it any more. I think this even as I am in Megan's car, being driven over there.

Ben wants me to come in to the ward with him so that we can see Grace together, once more.

Her eyes are closed. Every breath she takes bubbles loudly like a water cooler. She has no hair, no front teeth. But her face is washed clean, her skin translucent, unlined.

'Isn't she beautiful?' he says.

(viii)

Megan stays for a while. Once she's gone I just sit looking at Grace, letting the energy and dailiness of the world drain away. There's a book of psalms on the bedside table. I pick it up and leaf through the pages. I want to read her a psalm but I'm too shy to break the silence. Later, I think.

Something moves me to start stroking her arm. Grace opens her eyes. It's the first time I've seen her do this for a good few days. I get up and fetch the washcloth. She follows me with her eyes. I wipe her face, talking to her. I am wiping the back of her neck when her face contracts suddenly in a spasm of pain. She gives a little inward gasp of breath, then nothing. The breath doesn't seem to come out again.

I sit down beside her. I take hold of her hand. I wait. There is just silence. I am not in any hurry. I wait a little more. I look at my watch. It's 9.50 p.m. At last I go out and find one of the nurses. 'I think she's gone,' I say.

The nurse comes in and feels for a pulse. 'Oh Grace,' she says, very sweetly. 'Oh, Grace.'

(ix)

Although we've been expecting it – more or less – when at last it comes, the end feels bewilderingly flat. It's hard to comprehend the enormous switch between alive and not alive. Where is she? Her body lies in the hospital morgue for five days due to a tangle of paperwork, but her body is no longer the point. Her personality, her mind, her spirit, her *self*, has simply vanished: a terrible crescendo of confusion, struggle, panic, heart-battering fear and then – not peace, not transcendence – just a kind of clamp-lipped absence. Is that it?

People come to the house to pay their respects. One of the women sits with us for a long time, remembering the way

169

she and Grace and other women from these streets used to walk their children to school together in the mornings, thirty-five, forty years ago. 'It seems like yesterday,' she says to Ben. She talks about how everything has changed, and how her grandfather worked till he was seventy years old and never once in his life did he set foot on a bus or a vehicle of any kind, but always walked to whatever pit it might be, and once they were underground, they often had to walk miles and miles to get to the seam where they were working. 'But now ...'

Beverly calls in with a bunch of supermarket lilies, the special-offer label torn from the cellophane wrapping, and a card, which has a hurriedly scrawled message in one corner: 'So sorry to hear the news and if you ever need anything from over town or Tescos just let me know and I'm happy to drop in any shopping or anything you need.'

Eight days later the priest stands up in the little twelfth-century church where Grace spent so many Sundays and says: 'In the midst of life we are in death.' And we sit in the congregation of white and grey heads, drifting, dizzy, more than one foot in the other world, with all the people who have gone from here: Grace, Paul, and all the rest.

In a while we will pick ourselves up. We will return to the business of living, all the habits and routines, and work. But for now we're stupid and dazed, blunted by what we've seen. We've been down to the Valley where there is no light and no glory. It stops you in your tracks. It's like nothing I could ever have imagined.

ACKNOWLEDGEMENTS

Many of these stories have been published individually, in print or online.

'In the Current Climate' appeared on the Holland Park Press website in October 2015 as the winner of the 'I is Another' prize;

'Debts' was published in *Metropolitan* magazine, Manchester, 1996;

'Downsizing' was a finalist for the 1999 Asham Award and was published in the anthology *Reshape Whilst Damp*, Carol Buchan (ed.), Serpent's Tail, 2000;

'Escape Artist' was published in *Valentine's Day: Stories of Revenge*, Alice Thomas Ellis (ed.), Duckworth, 2000;

'Mistaken' appeared in 2015 in the online journal of the Australasian Association of Writing Programs (AAWP) *Meniscus*, vol. 2, issue 1;

'An Unplanned Event' was included in *The Mechanics Institute Review* #15 in 2018;

'Live Show, Drink Included' won the Chapter One International Short Story Prize and was published in *The Harvest*, Chapter One Promotions, 2010;

'Stranger' appeared in *New Writing 13*, Toby Litt and Ali Smith (eds), Picador, 2005, and was also translated into Mandarin and republished in the dual-language volume *A Little Nest of Pedagogues* by the British Council/Peking People's Publishing House, 2005;

An early version of 'Saucers of Sweets' appeared as 'Three Bloody Stories' in *Metropolitan* magazine, 1994;

'Rich' was shortlisted for the 2009 *Narrative* magazine Spring Contest but not published;

'Visitors' was a finalist in the 2009 Asham Award and was published in *Waving at the Gardener*, K. Pullinger (ed.), Bloomsbury, 2009;

'On the Way to the Church' appeared in *The Harvard Review* #52 in 2018;

'Into the Valley' was published in *The Harvard Review* #43, 2012.

Thank you to all the people who have sustained my writing over the years, especially to Elizabeth Baines and Ailsa Cox who first published my work in *Metropolitan* magazine in the UK, and Christina Thompson of *Harvard Review* who published me in the States; to my writing groups, past and present: Novelette Aldoni-Stewart, Lynn Foote, Dallas Sealey, Aoi Matsushima, Clare Bayley, Sue Healy, and in particular Annemarie Neary and Kathy Page who read and offered razor-sharp insights beyond the scope of both groups; to the memory of Gill Dennis, an inspiration and a wonderful teacher; to my patient family; and to Bernadette Jansen op de Haar who was willing to take a risk on these stories and give them a spine.

The Author

Vicky Grut was born in South Africa and lived in Madagascar and Italy before moving to England in 1980 to go to art school.

Her first short story was published in 1994 in *Metropolitan* magazine. Her work has appeared in new writing collections published by Picador, Granta, Duckworth, Serpents' Tail and Bloomsbury in the UK. Her nonfiction essay 'Into the Valley' (*Harvard Review* #43) was listed as one of the Notable Essays of 2012 in *Best American Essays 2013*.

She has been a lecturer in creative writing at the Open University, London South Bank and the University of Greenwich.

She is married to a Welshman from the Valleys and they have two sons.

More information is available from her website www.vickygrut.com.

Holland Park Press is a unique publishing initiative. Its aim is to promote poetry and literary fiction, and discover new writers. It specialises in contemporary English fiction and poetry, and translations of Dutch classics. It also gives contemporary Dutch writers the opportunity to be published in Dutch and English.

To

Learn more about Vicky Grut
Discover other interesting books
Read our unique Anglo-Dutch magazine
Find out how to submit your manuscript
Take part in one of our competitions

Visit www.hollandparkpress.co.uk

Bookshop: http://www.hollandparkpress.co.uk/books.php

Holland Park Press in the social media:

http://www.twitter.com/HollandParkPres
http://www.facebook.com/HollandParkPress
http://www.linkedin.com/company/holland-park-press
http://www.youtube.com/user/HollandParkPress
http://plus.google.com/+HollandParkPress